BAXTER MOON
Galactic Scout

John Zakour

Brown Barn Books
Weston, Connecticut

Brown Barn Books
A division of Pictures of Record, Inc.
119 Kettle Creek Road, Weston, CT 06883, U.S.A.
www.brownbarnbooks.com

Baxter Moon Galactic Scout
Copyright © 2008, by John Zakour

Original paperback edition

Library of Congress Control Number: 2007937369
ISBN: 978-0-9768126-9-2

Zakour, John

Baxter Moon, Galactic Scout: a novel by John Zakour

Printed in the United States of America

For my son Jay.

He's like Baxter, but cooler.

Also by John Zakour

Acknowledgements

I have to first of all give credit to my wife, Olga. After all, she's the one with the real job who supports me so I can write, write, write, hopefully getting a big deal someday.

I need to thank my agent Joshua Bilmes at JABberwocky Literary Agency for doing all those things agents do. I also need to thank Nancy Hammerslough from Brown Barn Books for all the work she put into Baxter.

Finally, I have to thank all the people who contributed (directly or indirectly) to characters in this book: Olga, Carolina, Natalia, Diego, Jose, Juan Ma, our dog Ebby and others I probably forgot.

Chapter 1

MY NAME, AND I'M NOT MAKING THIS UP, is Baxter Moon. I'm a second year space scout at the Galactic Academy of Scouts. We all call it GAS for short.

Before I came here, I was just plain Baxter Moon, happy-go-lucky kid. That was until the day I entered a video game contest playing Star Scout Seven-4D. Much to my surprise I won. Even more to my surprise, the grand prize was a full scholarship to the elite Galactic Academy. Second prize was a ten-meter, paper-thin screen, super-duper high definition TV. On a lot of days, I was pretty certain I got shafted mega time.

"Pull up, Baxter! Pull up!" GiS shouted, banging both his hands and his feet off the top of his head. If his face could have turned color, I'm sure it would have been beet red.

"I can do this," I said, slowly, with all the confidence I could muster.

I adjusted the pitch of my shuttle just a touch to the left. I held my breath and watched on the front view window as a rock-like asteroid, twice the size of our shuttle, slid by missing us by a paper's width.

Zenna and Elvin each breathed a little sigh of relief. It was nice to know my crew had such faith in me.

"You can't do this, Baxter!" GiS screeched. "It's too dangerous!" It was funny, when things were calm, GiS was always so prim and proper, well at least as prim as a chimp could be. Only as soon as things got a little dicey his calm, proper demeanor would go flying out the window.

"I can do this," I repeated. "I just need a little faith from my crew."

"I trust you, Baxter," Zenna said, as upbeat as ever.

While it was nice to have Zenna's support, her vote of confidence didn't exactly boost my confidence. Zenna is a great girl, like the sister that I never had. A sister that I get along with, I might add.

She's as strong as an ox. Well, actually four oxen. Certainly, if there is a fight I want her on my side. She also has a great feel for things mechanical and electrical. If it's broken she can fix it. If it's not broken she can improve it. Just don't ask her how she did it. She won't be able to explain.

The thing with Zenna is... How can I word this nicely? Let me put it this way. Mentally, she's slower than mega-thick molasses on Pluto. Whatever they did to Zenna to improve her physical strength made the part of her brain that processes certain bits of information not quite right. I guess nature likes to balance things out, no matter how much science tries to tip the scales one way or another.

I eased the shuttle's control joystick gently to the right. The left side of the ship lifted ever so slightly. Another couple of boulder-sized asteroids passed harmlessly underneath.

"This is not the proper action!" GiS insisted, hairy arms crossed over his chest.

"Cutting through this asteroid field saves us three hours on our trip," I insisted back.

"Yes, but only if we make it there alive," GiS said, being even more insistent.

"Details, details," I said with a smile. I was hoping that if I smiled enough, both my crew and I would have more faith in my judgment.

Elvin's fingers glided over his control screen as he entered some calculations. "Actually, we save three hours and twenty-two minutes," he said.

"See?" I said.

Elvin performed a few more calculations, running his fingers over the console so nimbly they were a blur. "Of course, we still have three thousand four hundred and seventy-seven more asteroids to avoid. Give or take one."

"That just happens to be my lucky number," I said.

Elvin looked at his screen. "I estimate there is a 1.3456 percent chance of success."

"That just happens to be my other lucky number," I said.

Elvin is Zenna's twin brother. While they may be twins by birth, or pseudo-birth in this case, they certainly aren't identical twins. In fact they are extreme-opposite, or anti-twins. While Zenna has dark hair, brown eyes and is tall and powerfully built, Elvin has light hair, green eyes and is short and definitely not powerfully built. On windy days back on Earth you could use him as an old-fashioned kite. Except for his agile fingers, he is the biggest klutz I have ever seen, and that's being kind. I've seen him fall out of bed when he was awake. I've seen him fall off a tricycle that wasn't moving. I've seen him trip and fall over a painted line on a floor. Though that time he claimed both his shoes were untied. When I pointed out his shoes had Velcro instead of laces, he noted studies showing how when loose, Velcro ties can be just as dangerous as laces. I didn't argue. I may not be the brightest laser in the tool kit, but I can recognize an argument I can't win.

On the up side, what Elvin lacks in muscle and coordination he makes up for in sheer brainpower. The dude is smart. If they cloned a new Einstein he'd be Elvin's student and Elvin would have to speak slowly to him. If I didn't know Elvin was flesh and blood (because I've seen him bleed so much) I'd swear he was a living, walking computer.

"Baxter, on September 7th, 2096, the day we started at the GAS, you told me your lucky number was 17. I remember it very clearly, it was around 13:05:04 and you were wearing that ripped green shirt with the holographic tongue. The one the commander hated so much."

"My lucky numbers change to match my mood," I said.

I pulled the control stick back rapidly, pulling the ship up. A jagged asteroid that had to be bigger than my parents' house, passed underneath us. I steadied the shuttle.

I saw two more massive asteroids coming toward us; one on the left, the other on the right. I rolled the shuttle to the side, slipping between them. I couldn't help but smile.

"Dive! Dive! Dive!" GiS shouted, while flailing his arms and legs and anything else he could flail.

"We're not in a submarine," I said, holding steady.

"I am your commanding officer," GiS said, which was kind of sad and scary, sad because it was true, scary because like I mentioned before, he's a chimp. Obviously, he isn't just any chimp. He's a genetically improved chimp. GiS is smarter than your average chimp. He's much smarter than your above-average chimp. In fact, he's smarter than most humans. The world classifies him as a *genetically improved simian* (or GiS). Still, to quote some dead old writer, *a chimp by another name is still a chimp.* Okay, maybe that's not the exact quote, but you get the idea. My boss is a chimp — literally. Sometimes I have a bit of trouble dealing with a commanding officer who is supposed to be lower than me on the evolutionary scale.

"I can't believe I have to take orders from a blooping monkey..." I mumbled under my breath. Thing is, I didn't mean to say it out loud at all.

GiS looked at me. "This is no time for you to go into one of your I-can't-believe-I'm-outranked-by-a-simian moods!" He looked at me, took a deep breath and then went into lecture mode. "First off, I'm not a monkey. I'm a chimpanzee. We come from totally different families. Chimps are larger and smarter than monkeys. My DNA is 97 percent the same as yours."

I jerked the shuttle to the side, barely avoiding a particularly nasty looking, jagged asteroid.

"I know. I just feel weird taking orders from somebody who wears a diaper," I said, keeping one eye on the view screen, but still nodding my head toward him.

GiS stood on his command chair and put his hands on his hips. He squinted at me, his forehead beetling. It was a look only an angry chimp could give. I knew he was fighting back the urge to jump up and down and hoot at me.

"For the hundredth time, Baxter..."

"Actually this is the hundredth and thirty-second time," Elvin corrected.

"For over the hundredth time," GiS continued, "this is *not* a diaper! It is an ultra low cut, form-fitting, pair of official simian uniform shorts." He looked up in the air with dignity. "Long pants are too warm and itchy!" he said. "They aren't designed for really hairy legs. Maybe your bald legs..." He put his leg out and bent it backwards and forwards and over his head, looking at it admiringly. "Plus, these allow me full flexibility," he said.

"You've made your point," I said, as I pitched the shuttle every so slightly to the left.

"Besides, Baxter, GiS is older than we are," Zenna, always the peacemaker, added. "He's not even a teenager anymore."

"Yes, that's another fine point," GiS agreed. "Not only am I chronologically older, but it's a proven fact that chimps mature faster than humans."

Those were all good points. That still didn't mean I had to accept them. "Okay, you're smart and you outrank me. I understand that, but that still doesn't mean I'm wrong!" I asserted, keeping one eye on GiS and the other on the view screen and windows. "I'm Sigma-II Squad's pilot. You have to trust my instincts!"

"Just as you need to trust mine," GiS said. "After all, as you like to point out, I am a chimp. Instinct is one of the many things we excel at."

"Yeah, that and eating bananas," I said without thinking. Talking without thinking is one of my bad habits. I'm hoping I'll grow out of it. Of course the way my day was going I wasn't sure I was going to live long enough to outgrow anything.

I quickly turned away to focus my attention on the hail of asteroids that were coming toward us. I didn't need to look at GiS to know he was glaring at me. I felt his angry gaze on the back of my neck. I couldn't worry about that now. I needed to keep both eyes glued to the navigation window at the front of the shuttle. The window showed nothing but a bunch of deadly rocks, so congested the screen almost looked as if it was one giant rock. The nice thing about flying a shuttle, though, is we're not limited to what we can see out the front window. The front of the shuttle is lined with view screens that show what's happening around us from every conceivable angle. I scanned over the screens; frantically searching for any crack in this wall of space rock. Little rocks would be no big problem, the shuttle's shields would handle those. I wasn't even worried about the huge rocks — the planet killers. Sure they could splatter us like a bug under a size 16 shoe, but they were so big I knew I could maneuver around them. The things that made the hair on the back of my neck stand at attention were the midsized asteroids. They could be anywhere from the size of a big watermelon to the size of a whale. If one of those hit us, that would be major trouble. I wasn't about to let that happen. I scanned the view screens again, looking for my opening. I noticed a small space in a barrage of rocks just to the left of us.

I tilted the control stick to the left and pushed down just a nudge. The shuttle dipped. A huge, spiked asteroid that looked like a metallic porcupine passed overhead. I had to time this right.

I squeezed the thrust button, just a pinch.

The shuttle's engine gave a quick extra burst. The shuttle jumped forward. I dipped the head just so slightly. I could see there was a huge, triangular rock jetting toward us. I needed to make sure the porcupine rock had completely passed over, before I dodged the triangle. Pulling this off it was going to take a lot of skill and even more luck.

Suddenly, the ship started to spin. Red warning lights started to flash. It's never a good sign when red lights flash.

"Uh oh," Elvin said, looking at a control panel. "That last one nipped our tail. Control will be reduced 55.55 percent."

"Great! Just what we need when we are trying to navigate through an asteroid field!" GiS said, arms and legs crossed. "You should have listened to me!"

"Not helping here, GiS," I shouted as I struggled to keep the shuttle steady.

The triangular space rock was barreling straight at us. I didn't have the controls to maneuver around it. I had to go to plan B and fast. The only problem was I didn't have a plan B.

The killer rock was growing bigger and bigger on our view screen. This called for a desperate measure. I popped the safety cover off the control stick's red fire trigger. "I'm opening up fire now!" I shouted, squeezing the trigger, not once but three times. When in doubt go for the overkill.

"No," GiS shouted.

It was too late. The energy bursts from the nose of our shuttle hit the approaching rock dead on. The laser blasts shattered the one big, deadly rock coming toward us at breakneck speed, into a lot more than one, not-quite-so-big-but-still-quite-deadly-rocks zooming toward us at break-pretty-much-everything speed.

I knew this would happen, but I was sure the shields could take it.

"The shields can take this barrage. Right?" I asked.

"I wish you'd asked me that before you fired," Elvin said, concentrating on the numbers flashing across his control panel. "The shields were built to handle a few asteroids hitting us. I estimate we are about to be hit by over three thousand asteroids. The sheer numbers will cause the shields to overload..."

"Oh great, *now* you tell me," I said.

The shuttle rocked with the collisions. I fought to maintain control. Smoke started pouring out of both GiS's and Elvin's control panels.

"Navigation, shields and drive are down!" Elvin shouted. "This is only the beginning — of the end!"

A warning siren started to blare all around us. I guess that was just in case we didn't notice the smoke and the flashing lights.

Elvin looked at his panel and shook his head. "We've taken hull damage," he looked at his screen, "everywhere!" he said.

"Could you be a bit more specific?" I asked.

He shook his head. "I could, but it won't matter." He pointed to the main window, which was unfortunately still quite functional.

I gulped.

There was a monstrous, mother of all asteroids bearing down on us. It had *splat* written all over it. Even though it had to be a few hundred kilometers away, it still dominated the window and all the view screens. Without navigation there was no way I could avoid it.

"Not good. Not good at all," I said.

"I still have faith in you, Baxter," Zenna said.

I was glad somebody did. I had maybe five tics to think of something. The first thing that popped into my mind was, "Mega-bloop, I'm dumb!" While that may have been true, it wasn't especially helpful. Another thought jumped into my brain. It was a desperate thought. But it was all I had.

"The tractor beam!" I said. "It's still functional. Right?"

Elvin glanced down at one of the gauges on his panel. "Yes, tractor beam is still functional."

"Great! We're not space dust yet!" I said.

"Baxter, I know physics isn't your strong point," Elvin said slowly, "but tractor beams bring things *toward* us." He pointed to the screen. "That thing is already barreling toward us!"

"Yes, but if we reverse the polarization of the beam, I'm betting we can use it as a pool stick, to bump the asteroid over us," I said.

"That could work," Elvin said.

I looked over at Zenna, who was already bent down under the control panel working away.

"How long will it take you to reverse the beam, Zenna?"

Zenna studied the panel. "At least thirty seconds."

"How long before impact?" I asked.

"Exactly twenty-nine seconds," Elvin said.

"Oh, that's just not going to work," I sighed.

GiS shook his head. "Well, at least you still have your amazing math skills," GiS said, not even trying to hide the sarcasm in his voice.

I looked up at the view screen, still totally filled by the image of rocks. I wanted to take my eyes off the screen, but I couldn't. It was like a bad hover-car wreck — you don't want to look at it, but you can't help yourself. We were as good as squashed. I braced for impact. Not that it was really going to make much of a difference.

"Simulation off!" a voice yelled.

The red lights stopped flashing. The smoke cleared. The blaring stopped. Everything around us, except for our chairs, faded away. The next thing I knew, my crew and I were sitting in the simulation room. Without all the holograms active, it was just a small boring room with yellow reflective lines crisscrossing its walls.

Commander Jasmine's voice boomed in over the loudspeaker. "Scout Baxter Moon, please report to my office immediately." You didn't have to be nearly as bright as Elvin to tell she was angry — extremely angry.

I fought back a gulp as I stood up from my chair.

I nodded to my crew and made my way to the door. As I left I heard the others talking.

"I'm actually impressed. He lasted 12.4 tics longer than I calculated he would," Elvin said, missing the point that we still failed.

"He should have listened to me and we'd all still be alive," GiS said, seemingly missing the point that it was a simulation and we were alive.

"I still have faith in him," Zenna said, seemingly missing the point that if it wasn't a simulation we wouldn't be alive.

Chapter 2

THE WALK THROUGH THE STATION'S transparent corridors from simulator room 7S to the commander's office wasn't far, but it was still one of the longest in my life. Of course I was walking slowly, taking in the sights. I was in no hurry to get there.

I knew I'd messed up, mega time. I also knew I'd done some pretty dumb things during my stay here. I once convinced Beta Squad that they didn't have to report to duty on any day of the week that has a vowel in its name. I once super-duper glued Kappa-III Squad's door shut making them late for roll call. Then there was that time I programmed the Station's old computer system to burp every five minutes. But cutting through an asteroid field, killing my crew, and losing my shuttle, even in a simulation, that was going to be frowned on.

I just wanted to get lost. But on a computerized space station that was pretty much next to impossible.

"Scout Moon, at your current rate of speed you won't reach the commander's office for another four minutes and seven seconds," said SC-711, the station's all-knowing, ever-present computer system.

"I'm getting there. I'm getting there."

"The commander is angry enough at what you did. I would not compound her anger by dilly-dallying."

"Dilly-dallying? You're one of the most advanced computers known to man or alien and you use the phrase, *dilly-dallying*?"

"There are eight other words I could have used, but with analysis of your posture along with computation of your ETA, dilly-dallying seemed to be the most appropriate for the occasion," SC-711 said.

"I'm a pilot. I don't dilly-dally," I said. I continued to walk slowly down the long hallway. The commander's office door was now in sight.

"Oh please," SC-711 said. "You are dilly-dallying while talking about dilly-dallying. The commander's anger will not be inversely proportional to the time it takes you to get there. The longer you take, the more she steams. The more she steams the hotter she gets. It's pretty much basic human biopsychology."

I had to admit, just not out loud, SC had a point. Letting the commander simmer in her own steam wouldn't help my case. I picked up the pace. I figured I was in for a mental spanking at the very least. I might as well get it out of the way.

Finally reaching the door, I took a deep breath. I took another deep breath. Sometimes I wasn't sure what in the universe I was doing here. Everybody else here was either the best of the best, or genetically improved to be special at something.

Except, of course, for Betas who were the worst of the worst. But even they had their place here. Some team of government social scientists somewhere decided that mixing the worst students in with the best would be "mutually beneficial to all." I guess if you're a scientist it's acceptable to be redundant. It makes things sound more proven if you repeat yourself only with different words.

Anyway, their theory is that the bright students' brightness will rub off on the dim students. The dim students will then become more useful members of society. These scientists (who obviously don't get out of the lab much) also figure that the rubbing off goes both ways. They surmise that some of the Betas' worst traits will rub off on the others around them, creating more humble people. This doesn't make much sense to me, but what the bloop do I know? I'm just a kid. An average kid.

I lifted my hand to knock on the door.

"Come in, Mr. Moon," Commander Jasmine called from behind the door, before I had a chance to knock.

The door popped open.

There she stood. Well, actually sat, before me, Commander Gloria Jasmine. Now, those who know me know I'm not prone to exaggeration, but I have to say that Commander Gloria Jasmine is the most beautiful woman I have ever seen. Okay, I'm only sixteen and haven't been paying attention to women for a lot of time. But even so, I think I can safely say that Commander Jasmine will be the most beautiful woman I will ever see, even if I live to be four hundred. She makes me wish I was older.

She's *that* good looking. I would say she's *that* hot, only that would be disrespectful to a superior officer. Plus, the commander is also a powerful MB, a mind bender. The last scout that let his mind wander to where teenage boys' minds wander, ended up quacking like a duck for the better part of a week. I had to compose myself and be careful with my thoughts. It wasn't easy. She might not have been perfect, but if there was a flaw you'd need a subelectronic microscope to find it. Her creamy golden skin, golden hair that flowed and curled just over her shoulders, her hypnotic green eyes, her smile, her legs, her…well, her everything. On those rare occasions when she smiled at me, I swore I could hear music playing.

"Come in, Mr. Moon," she said, more sharply than before.

I took a deep breath and walked in. The commander's office was very military. The walls and floors were spotless; she must have the cleaning bots whitewash them hourly. Her desk sat at the far end of the room near the wall in front of the world flag. The desk didn't have so much as a paper clip on top of its built-in information screen. Around the desk there were a few old-fashioned chairs, so straight they looked like they were standing at attention. The walls were dotted with perfectly aligned holo-pictures: the commander graduating from the academy, the commander graduating from medical school, the commander meeting the world president, the commander at the helm of a shuttle. It was pretty easy to see the theme. She pointed to a wooden chair in front of her desk. "Sit," she ordered.

I did as I was told.

She looked at me. She shook her head. "Mr. Moon, Mr. Moon, Mr. Moon," she said.

My first instinct was to say, *what, what, what*, but I fought it back. I just dropped my head and lowered my eyes. I figured the less I looked at her, the less trouble I'd get into.

"Look at me, Scout Moon," she ordered.

So much for that theory. I looked up at her. I had never noticed what perfect lips she had before. They were like... Man, I had to get my mind back to business before the commander gave my mind the business.

"I know I blooped up," I said meekly.

"Do you know why?" she asked, raising an eyebrow. "And watch your language in front of an officer."

"If that wasn't a simulation, I would have killed myself and my crew," I said.

"Plus you would have destroyed a multi-million dollar shuttle," the commander added, as only a commander could.

I suppressed a gulp. I had to do something to defend myself fast or I'd be on the next shuttle back to Earth. If I ever left this place I wanted it to be on my terms.

"I did what I had thought I had to do," I said, quickly. "The mission specs said the crew we were sent to save only had four hours of air left. I thought cutting through the asteroid field would give us much needed time."

I paused, waiting for her reply. None came. So I went on.

"It was meant to be a learning experience. I did learn a valuable lesson. I'm sorry that I would have killed my crew and destroyed the shuttle but we can't be certain I would have done that in a real situation. I knew it was a simulation. I'm betting if it had been a live exercise, my crew and ship would be just as alive as they are now."

Okay, maybe it wasn't the best argument, but it was the best I could come up with on the spot. I usually think fast on my feet. The problem was around the commander my mind would fill with all sorts of thoughts that weren't at all helpful to the situation. They were thoughts about her eyes, her lips...her other parts...thoughts that could get me in trouble.

The commander just looked at me for a tic or two, though it seemed like an hour. She smiled, ever so slightly. It was a beautiful smile, it excited me some, but it scared me more.

"Crews die and ships get destroyed," she said softly. "I might not like it, but I accept it. It's a fact of scout and military life."

I sat back in my chair. I didn't really know where this was going. I figured I might as well be comfortable. At least as comfortable as I could around a beautiful woman who was my superior officer.

"Not only did you disobey your commanding officer, you argued with and insulted him," the commander said.

I lowered my eyes. She had me on that one. I wanted to say, *he's a freaking chimp*. I didn't. No use making a bad situation worse. Chimp or not, like it or not, GiS was my superior officer. "I know I messed up mega bad," I said.

"Do I need to remind you again, Scout, that you are talking to a superior officer?" the commander said.

"I know I messed up, mega bad, sir," I said.

"Might I remind you, Scout, that I am a woman?" she said.

I really fought back the urge to say, *no need to remind me of that*. Instead I said, "Sorry, ma'am, I blooped up, mega bad, ma'am."

The commander just looked at me. I liked the attention, but wished it were for something other than me messing up.

"Mr. Moon, I know some people have trouble taking orders from animals. They don't think it's natural."

"It's not," I said.

"True," she said. "But just because something isn't thought of as natural doesn't mean it's not good. Studies have shown augmented animals are very loyal. They make great soldiers and officers. They work for less than humans."

"Have you ever served under one?" I asked.

She looked at me and smiled. Her smile sent shivers shooting straight down my spine into my toe nails.

"Yes, Baxter, I have. When I was in the space force fighter training, my CO was a skunk."

"You're kidding," I said.

She shook her head no. "I don't kid with scouts. The ironic thing was during martial arts training she'd always complain about my deodorant."

"Commander," SC-711 interrupted. "You have a message coming in from Earth Gov."

"I do?"

"I certainly have no need to make something like that up," SC-711 said. "It's a coded message and will begin in three minutes."

The commander squirmed a little in her seat. She wasn't quite flustered, but was the least calm and cool I'd ever seen her. She was trying hard not to let it show, though.

"In that case, Mr. Moon, we have to wrap this up fast."

I stood up. "I'll pack my bags."

"Sit!" she commanded.

I did.

She looked me right in the eyes. Bloop, she had beautiful eyes. Green had just become my favorite color.

"Baxter, pay attention," she ordered.

I snapped back out of my daze. I forced myself to concentrate on her words, not her face.

"Paying attention, sir, ma'am," I said in my most scout-like voice.

"You have talent as a pilot, just not as much as you think you have. At least not yet. If…"

"If I don't crash and burn," I interrupted.

She shook her head. "Yes, that goes without saying, as does not interrupting your commanding officer," she said.

I lowered my head. "Sorry, sir, ma'am."

"What I was going to say was, if you learn to be a better judge of your ability and also learn to trust those around you more, you may someday become as good as you think you are."

"So you're not sending me Earthside?" I asked.

"Not yet — you make things challenging for me," she smiled. "I like a good challenge."

"Thank you, sir, ma'am, sir," I said.

She pointed at me. "I warn you, though. I'm smart enough not to take on an impossible challenge. Another incident like this and you will be heading home. Got it?"

"Loud and clear, sir, ma'am."

"The call will begin in thirty tics," SC-711 said impatiently. "Scout Moon isn't cleared for this level call."

The commander pointed to the door. "Don't let me see you in here again, Scout."

I stood up. I gave her a little bow. "You won't, sir, ma'am."

I made a hasty exit from the room.

Chapter 3

"YOUR SQUAD IS IN THE COMMON ROOM," SC-711 told me. "If you hurry you may be able to help them to victory in a fooseball game with Kappa-II squad." I could have sworn there was a bit of urgency in SC-711's voice. He didn't want me anywhere near the commander's office.

He had no worries there. I didn't want to be anywhere near there either. I was just glad to get out of there not quacking like a duck.

As I walked, I peered out through the station's transparent walkway. The walkways that connect one section of the station to another are one of the most subzero parts of the place. They were totally transparent. You knew they were there because of the holographic wall markers that lined the walls, but you couldn't see the walls themselves. You were able to look through them and see millions and millions of stars all around you. It made me feel a part of something, yet kind of small at the same time. I can't really put my finger on it.

I let my mind wander a bit. I'm a kid. I can do that. It was funny. The commander had scolded me for thinking I was too

good for my own good. Yet before I went into her office I was wondering what the bloop I was doing here...I didn't think I was good enough. I hope when I get older I'll actually figure out what I'm good at and what my limits are. Maybe that's when you know when you're grown up. You know what you are good at. What your place in the universe is. Maybe.

I walked into the common room. It was packed to the rafters. Every second class squad from Alpha-II to Zeta-II was there, pilots, navigators and techs. (Except of course for the Betas. They aren't allowed to fly, so they work as maintenance support specialists.) The others were shooting the breeze at the space soda bar. Some were playing old-fashioned games like anti-grav ping-pong, fooseball or pinball-4D. Some were playing new virtual games like Jupiter-golf, full-contact bull roping and lawyer chomp. Others were just listening to the official space scout sanctioned tunes that included music from new groups like the Alpha Betas all the way to oldies like the Zappers to ancient bands like the Beatles. This was our time to relax, let loose a bit. The place was abuzz with the sound of kids being kids.

Somebody saw me. I think it was Dan Dankins, the mec for Delta squad. "Hey, it's Moon!" he shouted.

The room fell silent.

Zenna turned from her fooseball game and rushed over to me. She pulled me into a bear hug, lifting me off the ground.

"You're alive and still here!" she shouted. "I thought for sure the commander would either kill you or send you Earthside or both."

"Zen, if you don't let me down, I might not be alive much longer," I said, gasping for air.

She eased up on the hug. "Oops, sorry. Sometimes I forget my own strength."

She released her bear hug. I fell to my feet and took a deep breath.

Elvin walked over and patted me on the shoulder. "You don't think you're a dog or a penguin?" he asked.

I shook my head. "Nope, I just got a lecture. She got a rush call. I was saved by the bell. She didn't even get a chance to give me any demerits."

Kymm from Kappa-II squad walked over toward me. Kymm was Kappa's pilot. Their version of me, complete with attitude and all. She had long blonde hair, a little button nose and a nice smile, when she smiled. She was no Commander Jasmine, but then again, nobody is. She was still good looking, but I would never tell her that to her face. After all we were rivals. Friendly rivals, but rivals nevertheless.

Kymm gave me a little punch in the arm. She just loved flirting with me like that.

"Nice going, ace," she said. "You had the grand slam of simulated screw ups. Killing yourself, your crew, destroying your ship and irking off your commanding officer."

"When I do anything, even mess up, I do it mega time," I said.

"You've had enough practice at it," Kymm said.

Kymm may have been even cockier than me. Of course she had good reason. She was a bionic. Not a full-fledged half girl/half machine one like you see in sci-fi videos. She had small improvement chips (or ICs for short) planted in her eyes at birth. These chips let her see across a broader spectrum than non-augmented humans. She could see in the dark. She could see heat. She could even zoom in. At times I wished had improvement chips implanted in me, though most of the time I was glad I didn't. After all, this way when I did accomplish something I knew it was me doing it, not some chip. I can't help thinking when you start relying too much on chips that can be mass-produced you lose some of yourself. You lose a bit of your humanity. A bit of what makes you different from anybody else.

Kymm's navigator Chriz and her tech Lobi had walked over. They laughed.

"Yeah, nice going, Ace," Chriz said, mockingly. "Not even one of the Betas would be dense enough to go into that asteroid field! They don't call it the *field of sure death and total and absolute complete destruction* for nothing."

"Hey!" Elvin said. "Baxter lasted five minutes and ten tics in the field! That's a record!"

"Dead is dead," Lobi shot back quickly.

Kymm shot Lobi an angry look. "We all screw up from time to time. Even me," she said. "At least he had the guts to give it a try." Kymm looked at me and gave a slight, hardly detectable, smile. It was enough to make my heart skip a beat or two.

Lobi and Chriz both just backed away, like whipped pups.

"Thanks," I told Kymm.

"Don't mention it," she said. "Maybe you'll save me sometime," she said with a laugh. Yep, she couldn't help flirting with me.

Watching Kymm as she walked away, I tried to remind myself she was a fellow pilot, not a girl. Okay, with the long hair, that smile, those, well curves, she was a girl, there was no denying that, no matter how hard I tried. Still, she was a fellow pilot and rival first and girl second. I kept repeating to myself, she's a pilot, she's a pilot, she's a pilot.

Zenna tapped me on the shoulder, bringing back to the moment at hand. "I think there's somebody else you need to talk to," she said. She motioned, ever so unsubtly, with her head toward the corner of the room. Sitting there at a table was GiS. He was concentrating on his computer screen. He was pretending not to notice I had walked into the room. Zenna may not have been book smart, but when it came to common sense, she beat me hands down.

I made my way through the crowd over to GiS. He knew I was coming over but didn't acknowledge me. He wasn't going to make this easy. Chimps can really hold grudges.

"I should have done things differently," I said.

"You think?" he said sardonically without even looking up from his computer screen. "You mean the goal of that mission wasn't to destroy your ship and crew?"

"I shouldn't have argued with you," I said.

"Arguments are a part of the job," he said, still not looking up. "It's unnatural for humans and chimps to work together, so it's only natural we'd have our disagreements."

"Then why are you mad at me?" I asked, though I probably should know.

GiS still refused to look up from his screen. "Do I ever call you a baboon or an ape or an orangutan?" he asked.

"Not that I can remember," I answered.

"Then why did you call me a monkey?"

I hung my head. I had been doing that so much today I think my chin had left an indent on my neck.

"It was the heat of the moment. I spoke without thinking. I do that sometimes."

"You do that most times," GiS said, finally looking at me. Only now I wished he hadn't.

"Yeah," I said with a weak laugh. "It's a gift."

GiS looked at me and rolled his eyes. "If it's a gift, then it's a gag gift."

There was a moment of awkward silence.

"A good scout knows when to react without thinking and when to think without reacting," GiS said, using his most mentoring voice.

"You just love talking like that, don't you?" I said.

His angry expression turned to a more neutral one. "I guess I think it compensates for me being a chimp and all," he said.

"I'll try to be better," I said.

"No, you will be better," he corrected.

I held out my hand to shake. He shook my hand with his foot as only a chimp could.

"Apology accepted," he said. He looked at his wrist communicator. "You have judo class in five minutes. Don't be late."

I saluted and left.

All in all, that could have gone worse. I had made some huge blunders today and the day was still young. Hopefully I could chalk my mistakes up to experience. I'd certainly make mistakes again, but with luck they wouldn't be the same ones.

Chapter 4

I WENT TO THE LOCKER ROOM to change out of my official scout working uniform and into my official scout workout uniform. There really wasn't much of a difference between the two. They were both just jumpsuits with different names. Both of them were kind of an off-yellow color with stripes on the arms. The official brochure said the uniforms were "a golden color," but that was just a sad attempt to make them sound cooler than they were. The official working uniform had a slightly darker shade of yellow, ah, gold, patches around the bendable parts that covered the elbows, shoulders and knees. It was also made of non-wrinkle, non-flammable, stain-resistant, non-good-looking, hyperitchy, material called synthread. It was supposed to allow the skin to breathe. Both uniforms had my squad's sigma emblem on the left sleeve and my rank and duty on the right sleeve. I was actually surprised the uniform didn't come with a cape. Then we really would all look like dorky superhero wannabes.

The workout uniform was just a little more drab as it was a straight off-light-yellow color. It was also a lot more loose fitting and flexible. It was made of syncotton, a softer, less abrasive variant. It was much more comfortable and not quite as mega-dork-like. If it were up to me this would be my uniform of choice. I figure if you must look like a dork you might as well be comfortable. Of course, it wasn't up to me.

Elvin, Chriz and Lobi had beaten me to the locker room, which was par for the course. They had already changed into their workout uniforms. While they might have been prompt, they still weren't in a hurry to leave the locker area and hit the judo mats. The three of them would have much rather been in the simulator, bio lab, lecture hall or dentist's office than the gym. It was just how they were. They weren't physical kinds of guys.

"You guys can go in without me," I said as I slipped the top half of my uniform off over my head.

"No, that's alright, I'll wait for you," Elvin said. "After all, you are my pilot."

I looked at Chriz and Lobi. "What's your excuse?"

"We're being polite," Lobi said quickly. Lobi always did everything quickly. He was the type of kid that no matter where he was, he seemed to be in a hurry to get somewhere else. He reminded me of a confused ferret who'd had too much sugar.

"We're just afraid you'll get lost." Chriz said. "We know you're not too luminescent." Chriz was the anti-Lobi. He was cool and didn't do anything without thinking about it. He may not have been a super brain like Lobi or Elvin but he was still way smarter than the average dude and he knew it. He pointed to the clock on the ceiling. "You better hurry — we only have a minute to get out on the mats. I'm sure our pilot is already out there warming up."

I knew he was right. Kymm loved judo. I was also sure that Zenna was also out there. She enjoyed her judo time only slightly less than Kymm did. I didn't know what it meant that the girls enjoyed the judo far more than the guys. Then I thought about how rolling around the mats with Kymm was always fun. (Except for that time she kneed me, you know where.) That Kymm couldn't help flirting with me. I smiled. Yep, I bet she liked me as more than a fellow pilot.

Before I could ponder that for too long though, my train of thought was derailed by a cry from the room.

"Stop! What the bloop are you doing, you crazy Syn!"

"That's Kymm's voice," Lobi said nervously.

I slipped on my workout uniform top as I rushed toward the door that leads to the gym.

"Wait! You're not in full uniform!" Elvin shouted, not seeing the bigger picture here.

I ignored Elvin and entered the gym. Chriz was right on my heels. Neither of us liked what we saw.

Our judo instructor, Axel-248, had Kymm pinned to the ground by her throat. From the look of fear on Kymm's face, I knew this was no drill. Kymm was struggling to get free, but Axel-248 was too strong for her. In case you can't tell by the name, Axel-248 was an android. Of course the politically correct call them "synthetic people," or "syns" for short, SP for really short. SPs have gray skin and no eyebrows so you can easily distinguish them from regular, old-fashioned organic people. But truthfully, they are always so well built, muscular and chiseled looking that even if they didn't have the weird skin and no eyebrows, you'd still have to be denser than a black hole not to be able tell what they were.

A few years ago, some bigwig somewhere thought it would be wise to replace many of the organic instructors with SPs. They said this was because SPs were lower maintenance, had higher stamina and never complained about long hours and low pay. They were also supposed to be emotionless and consistent in their actions. Axel-248 had just tossed that theory out the window.

"Axel, what are you doing?" I shouted.

Axel, who had been glaring at Kymm, looked up from her at me. "Call me Sensei Axel!" he ordered.

"Sensei Axel, what are you doing?" I said.

"What the flying triple bloop does it look like I am doing?" he shouted. "I'm a teacher! I'm teaching her extreme self-defense!"

By this time GiS and Kymm's commander, K999 were in the room. K999 was a German Shepherd, the four-legged, canine kind. Even on his best days he was a bit of a grouch. (He always claimed that was because it was tough being without opposable thumbs in a world built for opposable thumbs.) Right now he was in a particularly nasty mood.

He was in bite-first-use-logic-later mode.

He leapt at Axel, mouth open, teeth showing. He meant business.

Unfortunately, so did Axel. As tough as K999 might be to normal humans, he wasn't much of a threat to a highly programmed but deranged android. Axel swatted K999 away with his free hand. The blow sent K999 flying across the room.

GiS had a different plan of attack. He, in true administrator form, called for help. He clicked on his wrist communicator.

"We need security to the main gym, stat!"

I looked at GiS. "Call security! That's the best you could come up with?"

GiS gave me his most dignified look. "We are no match for Axel. Security is armed. They will be able to stop him." He paused for a tic. "But it will take them four minutes to arrive."

"Four minutes!"

GiS shook his head. "They were on break. There's usually not any trouble here."

"But Kymm could be dead by then."

"So I suggest we provide a distraction," GiS said.

"Now that's something I can do!" I said.

"Me too," said Chriz.

"What about Lobi and me," Elvin asked. "What can we do?"

"I've often asked myself the same question," I said moving toward Kymm and Axel.

"Maybe we can distract Axel by getting him to try to compute pi to the last digit?" Lobi suggested.

"I got a better idea," I said. "Maybe I can make him mad!"

"Yes, no doubt you can," GiS said. "Let's just hope it helps."

I charged at Axel screaming, "Hyaaaaaaaaaaaaaaaaaaaaa!"

When I was within striking distance, I leapt at him. I was going to hit him with a flying kick to the head. I knew it wouldn't stop him, but I thought it might slow him down.

Axel of course saw the move coming from a light year away. He caught my leg in midflight. He tossed me back down to the ground.

"That was karate!" he scolded. "This is judo practice, Scout! Three demerits and no desert for you!"

"Don't you mean dessert?" I asked.

Axel shook his head. I swore I heard bolts rattling in there. "No, Mr. Smarty Scout, I mean desert. You will not be allowed to partake in our upcoming desert training exercise!" he barked.

If he thought that was a punishment he was even more deranged than I thought.

With Axel now concentrating on me, Chriz thought it was safe to attack. Chriz ran up to him, fired off a snap kick aimed directly between Axel's legs. The kick hit its mark. Axel just stood there, strangling away as Chriz fell over holding his kicking foot in pain.

Axel just shook his head. "I am a synthetic person, boy!" he shouted at Chriz. "I have no need for that part of my anatomy. Therefore I am not vulnerable to attack there. And if I were, I would have easily blocked your kick!" he ranted.

Zenna, who had been standing nearby, paralyzed by confusion, came over to me. She helped me off the ground.

"Careful, Baxter! Axel is super strong!" she said.

"I wish we knew somebody that was super strong that could help here," I told her.

Zenna gave me her deer in the headlights look. "Me too," she said. Suddenly it hit her. Her eyes opened wide. "Hey! I'm super strong!"

I gave her a little pat on the back. "Good, Zen," I said. "I'll try to keep his attention. You work your way behind him and pull him off of Kymm. We'll let security finish him off."

"Right!" Zenna said, accenting her word with a little salute. She took off, starting to creep behind Axel. Of course if this plan was to have a snowball on the sun's chance, I was going to have to do my part.

"What's going on, Axel?" I called.

Axel looked at me like I was speaking in Ancient Aquarian. "What do you mean what's going on?" he said, rolling his eyes. "What does it look like I am doing? I am still teaching judo and self-defense."

I pointed to Kymm pinned to the ground.

"Actually, it looks like you are killing Kymm," I said.

Axel shrugged. "It is not my fault that she is really bad at self-defense."

"Yes, it is. You're her instructor," I said. "Therefore if she's bad it's your fault. You should turn yourself off and perform a system bug diagnostic."

Axel looked up in the air for a tic. His eyes glowed red. He looked back at me, all the while never releasing his grip on Kymm.

"I just ran a very thorough test. All systems are functioning at peak, A1++ levels. I must therefore conclude that Kymm is simply a rotten pupil. Hence, therefore I must also conclude that I must give her the ultimate failing grade."

So much for my attempt at using straight logic on a twisted syn. I needed another idea and fast. Luckily, one popped into my head. Believe it or not, it was sparked from Lobi's stupid "compute pi to the last digit" remark. It just goes to show you never know where inspiration will come from. Of course to make the inspiration work, it was going to take some perspiration.

I moved slowly toward Axel, carefully calculating my words.

"Isn't your role as an instructor to instruct?" I asked.

Axel glanced at me for a tic. He looked at the struggling Kymm. He looked back at me. He shook his head like he was totally exasperated with me. "Yes, we've been through this, of course it is. Hence the reason the two words share a common root."

"A successful instructor must have students that can learn. Correct?" I said.

Axel closed one eye while he processed what I said. "Yes, I suppose that would be the optimal case," he said.

"If you kill Kymm she won't be able to learn anything," I said.

Axel looked at me hard. He looked up at the ceiling. He looked back at me.

"Hmm, yes, Student Scout Moon, that may be a valid point. But as far as I know, no scholars or studies have ever established that we stop learning after we die," Axel said in a professorial tone. "Perhaps we learn about different planes of existence?"

I fought off the urge to shake my head in confusion. I was having a philosophical conversation with a deranged android about after-life learning. Bloop, I needed a hobby!

"Even if there is after-life learning," I said, slowly, just trying to give Zen more time. "Chances are about one in gazillion that it would be about judo and self-defense."

"I don't believe gazillion is an actual number, therefore your argument is once again flawed, blemished and unsound," Axel said, thinking far more about my statement than he should have.

Zenna had now managed to work around behind Axel. I needed to keep him thinking a little more.

"I hate to break this to you, Axel, my big metal bud, but you're not really an expert on either numbers or the metaphysical."

Axel shook his head. "I have no more metal in me than you do," he said. He thought for a tic. "Actually, I have less. After all your blood contains iron and zinc. Mine doesn't. In fact..."

Axel didn't get to finish his statement as Zenna grabbed him. Zenna might not have been mentally fast, but physically she was like lightning on heavy-duty caffeine. Before Axel could do anything other than release his grip on Kymm, Zenna lifted him up in the air and slammed him, back first, to the ground. It was impressive. I had to remember not to make that girl mad.

I moved forward toward Kymm. I shielded her with my body.

"Are you okay, Kymm?"

"Took you long enough to get him off me," Kymm said with a weak whisper and a weaker smile.

"Save your thanks for later," I said. "We're not out of the asteroid field yet."

"Given your track record, I wish you had used a different analogy," Kymm whispered.

"Good point," I said, talking to Kymm but keeping my eyes on Axel and Zenna.

Zenna's move would have devastated a normal human, or, for that matter, a normal synthetic human; but Axel was neither. Axel was built to take and give out heavy-duty damage. He had withstood Zenna's best shot, but now he was set to return the favor.

Axel used a spinning leg sweep to take Zenna's legs out from under her, bringing her to the ground. He flipped himself up off the ground without using his hands. He stood over Zenna. He hesitated for a second. I could tell he was trying to decide which of us to attack now.

"What's wrong, big syn man?" I taunted. "Can't decide who you want to teach next?"

"This is not the way to treat your honored instructor," Axel said. "I am afraid I am going to have to give you all ten demerits, then kill you, then fail you."

"Man, you're a tough grader," I said.

That remark somehow caught Axel's attention. He forgot about the girls and zeroed in on me.

"That is untrue, a lie, a falsity," he said, angrily.

"Nice going, Ace," Kymm said. "Make the crazed, super android even crazier!"

"That's my plan," I said.

"You don't spend a lot of time planning your plans, do you?" Kymm said.

"Nah, planning my plans just slows me down," I said.

Axel moved toward me. He was trying to be cautious but his anger had gotten the best of him. (He probably wasn't programmed on how to handle anger.) "I'm going to give you the last judo lesson of your life," he said pointing at me.

For those of you who have never had an crazed android come at you with the goal of killing you, it's not a pleasant feeling. If I said I wasn't scared, I'd be lying through my teeth. My legs were trembling but I held my ground. Both the girls (and Chriz) were hurt. I had to keep Axel distracted a little longer.

"If I were you, I'd run now," I told Axel, in my manliest voice, just hoping it wouldn't squeak.

Axel just gave me a confident smile. "Why should I, the honored teacher, run from you, the pupil? You aren't even my best pupil. In fact you aren't in my top hundred pupils. In fact, you are a putrid puny pupil."

I pointed behind him. "If you run you might be able to throw off the security dudes behind you," I said.

Axel shook his head. "Yeah, right. Like I'm going to fall for that. That trick is almost as old as saying, look your sock is untied."

On that note, the guards behind Axel fired their energy weapons at him. The force of the beams split Axel in half. Both halves fell to the ground. Axel's bottom half just lay there harmlessly. His top half, though, was much more stubborn. It pushed itself up and glared at the guards.

"This is martial arts!" Axel shouted. "Energy weapons are cheating! I'll crush you, even if I have to do it with my teeth!" he screamed.

He charged at the guards on a his hands. He looked kind of like a crazed crab. It was either freaky or comical or just plain sad. I guess it depends on how you look at it.

The guards were taking the charge seriously. After all, a killer android is still a killer android, even if it's legless and, in this case, mostly mindless. Bloop, being mindless probably made Axel more dangerous.

The guards locked their laser sights on Axel. The red lights from the sights dotted Axel's broad forehead. He looked up at the dots cross-eyed. "Uh oh," he said. "This isn't good!! Not good at all!!! Blooping cheaters!!!! There are no guns in judo!!!!!"

Those were the last words Axel uttered before the guards unloaded their weapons on him, turning him into a pile of tomorrow's trash. Kind of sad, yet kind of fitting for the occasion.

GiS walked up to me. He gave me a little pat on the back with his foot as he looked at the scraps that used to be Axel. "Nice job, Scout," he said.

"Thanks," I said.

He pointed to my non-matching top and bottom of my uniform. "You are out of uniform, though." He turned and walked away. "I'll let it slide this time, but if it happens again it will be two demerits."

Chapter 5

THAT EVENING I ATE DINNER in my room. Normally, scouts are expected to eat together in the mess hall. It's another one of those things they tell us builds camaraderie. We are each allowed three exceptions per semester, as long as we have a good excuse. Luckily, the commander and GiS both felt being blown up in a simulator and then going mano-a-machino against a crazed android was legit, though just barely.

My roomies Elvin and Zenna were both excused too, but they decided to be good scouts and go eat in the mess. Elvin hadn't really done all that much in the fight, so I wasn't much impressed that he wanted to mess with the rest of the scouts. He probably wanted to take a survey on what the other squads thought of me. I had to give Zenna credit, though, she never let anything stop her or get her down. She didn't even need to go to the med center.

You may be thinking, wow — coed rooms! How subzero. Or you may be thinking, yuck — coed rooms! How megabarf. But once you get used to them they're no big deal at all. Like I said, I look at Zenna as my sister, one who can easily kick my butt. Besides, nobody ever sees anything they shouldn't. We have official white sleeping uniforms and the light blue relaxing uniforms we have to wear all the time when we're not in our other uniforms. (In case you haven't guessed by now this place is big on official uniforms.) If you need to change, you do so in the privacy of either the bathroom or the side changing room, which is basically just a closet with a different name.

"Scout Moon, you have a call coming in," SC-711 said.

"You're kidding," I said. It was extremely rare to get calls up here except on Sunday, the official "home phone" day.

"I do not kid," SC-711 said. "And if I did, it would certainly be something funnier than you have a call coming in..."

"Who's the call from?" I asked.

"I did not ask," SC-711 said.

"But I'm sure you still know," I said.

"True," SC-711 said.

"I'm not sure I want to talk," I said.

"I'm sure you do," SC-711 said.

The view screen lowered from the ceiling.

"It is Mom," SC-711 said, not giving me any choice.

My mom's image filled the video screen. She had dark brown hair, brown eyes and a dark complexion. A lot of people, well, most people, say I look like her.

Mom looked at me and smiled. "Hi, honey, you look tired." That's how Mom started every conversation with me. In this case I couldn't argue.

"I'm a bit tired, Mom. Why'd you call?"

"I was just thinking of you," she said. "I had a funny feeling that something was wrong."

I shook my head. "Nope, everything is fine," I said.

"One of my patients told me there was a little mishap up there today," Mom said. She was an Earth Force doctor, which gave her a few connections other moms didn't have. Today those connections were making my life more complicated. I didn't want to lie to my mom, but I also didn't want her to worry. I can handle myself.

I shook my head again. "Yeah, there was a little problem, but it's over with. It had nothing to do with me." I paused for a second. "How's Dad?"

"He's on location on Mars covering a story about a potential robot labor strike." Mom looked around the room. "Where are Elvin and Zenna?" she asked.

"At the mess, eating." I said.

"Why aren't you eating with your squad?" she asked in typical mom fashion. (At least if your mom is an officer in Earth Force.)

"Well..." I said slowly.

"Scout Baxter J. Moon, don't you dare lie to your mother and superior officer," she said, quickly. Mom wasn't big on being an officer, she considered herself a doctor who happened to work for Earth Force. Still, she didn't mind pulling rank on me if she thought it would accomplish something.

"Okay, maybe it had a little to do with me," I admitted.

Mom just looked at the screen. I couldn't see her foot but I was sure she was tapping it nervously.

"But I'm totally okay now," I said. "Some people even think I might have saved the day. I'm sure Elvin is down there now conducting a survey."

Mom smiled. "Remember, Baxter, you can never please everybody," she said. "Just make sure you remember to please yourself."

"What about pleasing my mom?" I asked.

"You never have to worry about that one," she said. "As long as you're happy, I'm happy."

"I'm happy, Mom. Tired, a little sore, but happy."

"Good, what about Elvin, Zenna and GiS?"

"They are all fine."

"How's that Kymm girl? She's a cute one."

"She's fine, too, and I haven't noticed."

"No lying to your mother, Scout Second Class, Baxter Moon."

"Yes, ma'am."

"Oh, tell GiS I just love that cornbread recipe he emailed me," Mom said.

"I can't, Mom," I said.

"Why not?"

"Because that's just too weird on too many levels," I said.

Luckily, before Mom said anything else, Elvin and Zenna came in. They were both laughing. I think that made my mom feel better.

"Man, Baxter, you were the talk of the mess," Elvin said. Zenna elbowed him in the ribs. She pointed to the vid-phone. Elvin stopped talking and starting thinking.

"Yes, they said it's amazing that you lead such a boring life," Elvin said, making a faint attempt to cover up. He looked up at the screen, pretending (poorly) just to notice it was on. "Oh, hi, Dr. Moon," he said.

"Hi, Mrs. Moon, ma'am" Zenna said, saluting. "You look lovely."

Mom just gave us one of her knowing mom smiles.

"I'll let you kids talk," she said. "I just wanted to check in. Love you," she said.

"Love you too, Mom," I said.

"I love you too, Mrs. Moon," Zenna said.

"I am very fond of you as a superior officer and a second mother figure in my life," Elvin said.

Mom blew us a kiss. The screen went blank.

Elvin went right back into spaz-squared mode. "Zappit, Baxter! You are the talk of the mess hall!" he said excitedly, barely able to contain himself. He reminded me a lot Lobi right now. Maybe they shared some DNA?

"Is that a good or bad thing?" I asked.

"Mostly good, 65.345 percent to be exact. Though some of the scouts think you engineered the whole ordeal to make yourself look good."

"Yeah, like I'm smart enough to pull something like that off," I said.

Elvin nodded in agreement. "That's what I told them!" he said.

Zenna sat down on her bed and pulled one of her boots off. She sniffed it. "Phew, these super-duper odor zappers seem to work," she said with a smile of relief.

"Obviously, since Baxter and I are still standing," Elvin said, only half kidding.

"Sorry, one of the down sides of having super strength is super foot odor," she said as if Elvin and I weren't already well aware of that.

Zenna took off the other boot. She sniffed it, just to be on the super safe side. She smiled again.

"Chances are roughly 99.99 to 1 that if the right one doesn't smell neither will the left one," Elvin said.

"A girl can never be too careful," she said. "I guess it's unlady-like to knock people over with foot odor."

"So what did people think about the cause of the incident?" I asked, desperately trying to steer the conversation away from Zenna's potential foot odor.

"Besides the ones who thought you caused it?" Elvin said.

"Yes, besides those."

"Some think the TVTrons did it!" Zenna said. Now she was getting excited.

"The TVTrons?" I said.

For those of you who don't know, the TVTrons are a group of semi-intelligent, automated machines that roam the galaxy, turning people into zombies and forcing them to be entertained. They don't really call themselves TVTrons, they refer to themselves as Universal Electronic Entertainment Devices, or UEEDS. We Earthlings have nicknamed them TVTrons; it just seems more fitting. They don't appear to be all that menacing. Actually, they look pretty ridiculous, like bizarre, old-fashioned TV sets on wheels, with robot arms on their sides. Their simple looks can be deceiving, though, because they emit some sort of radiation from their screens that drains their victims of their mental and physical energy; forcing the victims to mindlessly watch them — forever, or until they starve to death, whichever comes first. So far only deep space miners have had any problems with them. The TVTrons seem to wander around the galaxy mindlessly looking for victims or "test markets" as they call them.

"This doesn't seem like the work of TVTrons," I said. "Not their style."

"Styles change," Zenna said. "Maybe they have too."

"One of my theories is they've developed a virus that infects our machines," Elvin said. "They want to turn our machines against us. Then they think we'll be forced to turn to them for all our entertainment and educational needs."

"And you come up with this how?"

Elvin pointed to his head. "Remember, I think like a machine," he said proudly.

"Interesting point," I said as I plopped down on my bed. Though it wasn't really all that interesting. I just didn't want to talk about it any longer. I've learned the quickest way to end a conversation with Elvin is just to agree with him. Who knows? Maybe his theory was right. In an infinite universe I guess anything is possible no matter how whacked out it might seem. Bloop, I had a chimp for a boss, one roommate who'd rather compute pi than eat pie and another whose foot odor once KOed an entire shoe store.

I closed my eyes and tried to turn my brain off. It had been a long, weird day. One of the strangest days of my life. I realize I'm not all that old, but I was hoping that even if I lived to a ripe old age, today would rank in my top ten of bizarre days. Unfortunately, I had the uneasy feeling that things were just going to get weirder.

Chapter 6

THE NEXT THING I KNEW, Zenna was shaking me. Actually she was shaking the entire bed by lifting it up with one hand and then dropping it.

"Baxter! Baxter, wake up!" she said.

"Why?" I said half-dazed. "Is it time to go to bed?"

"No," she said. "You just fell asleep there last night. We didn't want to wake you, you looked so content, but we have astrophysics in thirty minutes."

"And you're kind of ripe smelling," Elvin added. "If you're late for another class, GiS will go ape on you." He waited for a second, then he just had to say it. "Get it? Go ape."

I sat up in bed. "I get it."

"I don't," Zenna said.

I rolled out of bed and headed toward the shower.

"I'll meet you guys in the lecture room," I called back.

"Actually," SC-711 said. "You need to report to the commander's office."

I looked at the room's ceiling speaker that was broadcasting SC-711's voice.

"Why?" I asked. "What have I done now?"

"I do not know. It is not my function to ask for information, just to give information," the speaker replied.

"Come on, SC-711, you're holding back something," I said. "Nothing goes on here without you knowing about it."

"Flattery will not work on me. I have no ego. Or for that matter an Id. Or for..."

"Not trying to flatter you. I'm just stating a fact."

There was a pause. I could tell SC-711 was processing.

"I do not believe you are in trouble," he said. "I only know the commander needs to see Sigma-II and Kappa-II squads in her office."

"Well, if Kappa is going to be there too, it can't be too bad," I said. At least I hoped it was true. I jumped in the shower. I didn't know what was coming up, but at least I'd smell good.

Chapter 7

OF COURSE I WAS THE LAST ONE to report to Commander
Jasmine's office. GiS, Elvin, Zenna, K999, Kymm, Chriz
and Lobi were all standing at attention in front of her desk. The
commander was the first to notice me enter the room.

"Nice of you to join us," she said.

GiS shot me a glare.

"Galactic Scout Second Class Baxter Moon reporting,
ma'am," I said.

"Late as always," Chriz said under his breath, but loud
enough for everybody to hear.

"No, he had a full three tics to spare," the commander
said.

"Actually, three point five tics," Elvin corrected without
thinking.

The commander shot him a glare. Elvin sank back in terror.
For a tic I thought he might even start to suck his thumb.

The commander straightened up and turned her attention
back to all of us. She was even stiffer, more business-like than

normal. (Though she still looked beautiful.) I knew something was up. I was just hoping it wasn't something I caused.

"What do you know about the Aquarians?" she said.

Everybody but me raised a hand, paw or a foot. Elvin and Lobi each raised two hands.

The commander looked right at me. "Scout Moon?" she said with a raised eyebrow.

"They're the only other race of humanoids we've run into so far in our interplanetary travels. They look pretty much like we do only they have blue skin, probably due to the chemicals in their atmosphere. Despite the fact that their planet is 72 percent land, they still call it Aqua. Of course that might just be a weird kink in common translator programs." I was proud of myself for knowing all that.

"Anything else?" she asked.

Everybody else raised a hand, or something like a hand.

"Anything else, Scout Moon?" she asked.

"They come from a planet in the Sirius D system. A system we didn't even discover until a few decades ago. It's about ten light years away and not all that bright a star."

"That's just so rudimentary," Chriz mumbled.

The commander and K999 both gave him a look. Chriz shrank back a step and quivered.

"Anything else?" she prompted me.

"They don't trust us much, and we don't trust them any more than they trust us," I said. "We've had very little contact with them."

The commander smiled. "That is until last week," she said. "Both our planets are interested in establishing trade relationships. It seems they have a fondness for our chocolate chunk cookies. We sent a ship of our council members to meet with and negotiate with a ship of their politicians in a neutral system, Sirius C minor."

There was silence while the commander let what she said sink in.

"If it turned out well, I doubt we'd be here now," I said, not bothering to let anything sink in.

The commander smiled at me. It wasn't a happy smile though.

"That is correct, Scout Moon. Contact has been lost with both ships." She paused to catch her breath. "They of course blame us. We of course blame them. If something isn't done soon, we could be on the brink of full-scale, intergalactic war. A war neither side could win."

"Does anybody ever win a war?" I asked.

GiS shot me a look, but the commander just smiled.

"No, I guess not," she said earnestly. "But in this war the losses would be even greater."

Once again everybody stood there in silence. Once again I broke the silence.

"Excuse me, Sir, ma'am, but how does this concern us? We're just bunch of Scouts, Second Class," I said, even though I had a sneaking suspicion already. I hoped I was wrong. They couldn't have been thinking what I thought they were thinking.

"We want your squads to go to Sirius C and see if you can find any survivors."

"What?" everybody except me blurted out.

"It is our hope that you can find out what happened and avert a war," the commander said.

"These kids aren't soldiers, Commander," K999 said.

"Exactly," the commander said. "After what just happened, the Aquarians would not hear of us sending soldiers into neutral space. They would treat it as an act of war. As would we if they did the same thing."

"That doesn't make a lot of sense," I said.

"Politicians rarely do," the commander said, bluntly.

"But these kids are only second class!" GiS said. "Why not send the first class scouts?"

The commander shook her head. "Because the first class scouts are 17 to 18 years old and have been certified with deadly arms. The Aquarians would have none of that."

"But..." GiS started to say.

"Don't you have faith in your squad?" the commander asked.

"Of course I do," GiS answered with surprising confidence. "It's just they are young. Not fully trained."

"They know how to fly and how to rescue ships. That's what we want here," the commander said.

The commander looked at us all. "I'm not going to beat around the launch pad, scouts. This is a very dangerous mission. Anybody who would like to back down, just say so, and we will get another squad to replace you. You were my top choices, but there are other fine squads that could work nearly as well."

Nobody said anything, although I was sorely tempted.

The commander smiled. This time it was a smile she felt. "Good. You will take your scout ships into orbit around Mars. There you will dock with the intergalactic starsphere Searcher 0.5. Searcher will be run by SC-711 and a team of bots. It will take you to the Sirius C system. Any questions?"

"The incident with Axel yesterday, was that some kind of planned test?" I asked.

The commander shook her head. "No, that was just a strange coincidence. I had Sigma-II squad picked as one of my top three squads. Your performance yesterday convinced me you think fast on your feet. That will be handy here."

The commander looked us all over. "I am very proud of you all. I know you will make your entire planet just as proud," she said.

Man, no pressure there, I thought to myself.

"You are dismissed," the commander said.

Everybody else turned to leave the room. I stood there for a tic. I had another question.

"*I wouldn't be sending you unless I thought you could succeed, Scout Moon,*" the commander said inside my brain.

I decided it was best not to question somebody who could place her thoughts in my head. Was that another sign that I was becoming more mature? I turned and followed my crew out the door.

Chapter 8

WHEN WE REACHED THE SHUTTLE BAY, Alpha-I squad was just leaving. You didn't have to be an expert in human behavior to tell they weren't happy about it. They must have been tuning up their shuttles and didn't like the idea of having to leave the bay, especially for second class students.

Alano, Andi and Andra, were all big, blonde and blue eyed. They were triplets, all GI, genetically improved. If Andra didn't have breasts, I'd be hard pressed to tell her apart from Alano and Andi. They looked like grownups compared to us. I wasn't sure why we were going and they weren't. I knew what the commander had said, but I couldn't help thinking that we were going because we were more expendable.

Alano came over and gave GiS a polite if not heartfelt little salute.

"Alpha-I clearing the deck as ordered, sir," he said, in almost robotic tone.

"Very good, Alpha-I," GiS said.

You could see it in their nonblemished faces that they were thinking the same thing as I was. *Why are they here?* They were of course too good scouts to question authority, but it was eating them up inside. Remember how I said with GIs there is always a tradeoff? They gain something but lose something else. With Alpha-Is, the thing they lost was some of their humility. It was still in there. There just wasn't very much of it and they didn't let it out all that often. Like Andra told me once when she crushed me in a fooseball game, "It's hard to be humble when you are as good as we are."

As soon as Alpha-I cleared the area, GiS entered his access code into the shuttle bay's entry door. He put his foot up on the door's DNA scanner.

"Due to extra security of this mission, please enter security confirmation phrase," the door said.

GiS stood there for a tic just staring at the door.

"You do remember your phrase," I said to GiS.

"Of course he remembers," Zenna said. "GiS has an excellent memory. He never forgets one of our birthdays." She looked at him looking at the big metallic door. "You do remember the code. Right?"

GiS dropped his head. "I remember it," he said softly.

"Please enter extra security phrase," the door repeated, this time it sounded a bit uppity.

"Bananas, Bananas, here and there. Bananas, Bananas everywhere. I love to eat them day or night. Bananas, Bananas are out of sight…" GiS said meekly.

I looked at him. He looked at me. He pointed at me. "Not one word!"

I put my hand over my mouth. If we survived this mission I was going to have to give GiS a hard time about that. Only right now wasn't the time. We had a job to do and we couldn't let anything distract us.

"Phrase verified," the door chirped, sounding like we had just made its day. "Have a nice flight and remember to always harness up. It's not just a good idea, it's also regulation 13, section 23 c.

The door recessed into the wall.

We all entered the shuttle bay.

I can safely say the shuttle bay is my favorite place in the station. I really like the rec room. My dorm room is okay. On a good day (when they aren't serving Hungarian rehashed hash), the mess hall can be alright. The astrolab and simulators are cool. But the shuttle bay rocks my socks off!

You wouldn't think much of it to look at it. It was a big round open area with a dozen huge doors each positioned exactly 30 degrees from each other. The bay was kind of like a glorified warehouse that happened to be located on the bottom section of a space station. Twelve shuttles could launch or land here at once. There was no place on the station I would rather be.

GiS always said that I had space dust in my blood. That's probably why I liked it here so much. That's the reason he thought I had potential to be a great pilot. He'd also say that I'd let that space dust clog my ears and my brain. That's the reason he wasn't sure I would ever reach that potential. That's GiS — he can't give a compliment without balancing it with a critique. I guess it makes him feel all sage and useful.

The bay was huge, as big as any two stadiums I had ever seen. You could play a couple of anti-grav soccer games inside of it without either interfering with the other. Across the bay I could see both our and Kappa's shuttles. They were up on elevated landing pads being tuned by numerous little vacuum-cleaner-sized bots zooming around this way and that way. They were like a hyper-electronic pit crew.

A tram cart rolled over to us. "Would you like a lift to your shuttles?" the cart asked in a happy, but metallic, voice. This was different. Normally, all classes except First must walk to their shuttles. It's considered a good way to build character.

"We'll walk," K999 answered for all of us. Apparently we still needed some character building.

As we walked toward the shuttles I couldn't help thinking about my feelings toward that machine. It's not love. At least it's not the same kind of love I have for my mom and dad. It's not like the kind of love I have for my dog Pooper (hey, I named him when I was four). It's also different from the kind of love I have for my crew. They might get on my nerves from time to time, but I would do anything for them. It's surely different from the feeling I have for certain girls, say Kymm, but I'm not even going to go there. My shuttle, my ship, I can't explain my feelings for it. It's a machine. I don't think I can love a machine. Bloop, I don't want to love a machine. That's just plain wrong. They have help groups for people like that. My relationship with my shuttle is different. When I get in and take the control stick in my hand, it's like the shuttle and I become one. It's a hard feeling to explain, especially if you're not a pilot.

I talked about it once with Kymm. I was sure she'd make some crack about how the control stick was a substitute for something I was lacking in my manhood — and she did. She couldn't resist the dig, though I know she's just doing it to cover up her attraction to me. After that, though, she admitted she felt the same way. Though she didn't think she had the same passion for it than I did. She, of course, put in another dig about my manhood. Kymm, like GiS, couldn't give me something without taking something back. It was part of her nature and part of our rivalry. I guess it was just one of those life tradeoffs.

After a few minutes, we reached the shuttle. It was about the size of the old-fashioned school bus you see in museums. In fact, some people even called them "space buses" as they had the same rounded look to them. I always thought they looked like a cross between a speed boat and a bus with short rounded wings. They were meant to be functional, not pretty. Still, I found the look pleasing in an aerodynamic sort of way. (I guess on some level I'm as geeky as Elvin.) There was a ramp that led from the floor to the landing pad. I walked up the ramp to the shuttle door.

I gave the shuttle, my shuttle, a pat on the side.

"You do know it is only a machine," Kymm called as she walked by toward her shuttle.

"Yep, I know," I said. "Still, it doesn't matter."

She grinned.

I opened the door and walked in. My squad followed. They were much more business-like, much less excited than I was.

The back part of the shuttle was open, reserved for cargo or anything else we needed to carry. It had pop-up seats that were usually stored under the floor. If you needed them, they were available with the push of a button.

The navigator's control console was near the front on the left side of the shuttle. The engineer's control console and panel were on the front right side. The walls next to each console were lined with information screens. They could show anything from the status of the ship's engines to any view of what was outside from any angle. Once, much to GiS's chagrin, Elvin even programmed them so they would give me highlights of the Mets' game.

Elvin and Zenna quickly moved to their seats. They started taking readings.

The pilot's and squad commander's seats were located next to each other, near the front of the shuttle. This gave a good clear view of the shuttle's front window and the panoramic view screens located above and below the window. I moved slowly toward my seat. I wanted to savor the moment.

The seats were big and comfy and could swivel 360 degrees, and tilt 180 degrees. You can actually spin them so fast you can make yourself barf. (Trust me, I'm speaking from experience.) Both seats had control panels on the left and right arms. It didn't matter which one you used. Both panels were fully programmable. The arms of the chair were also lined with control buttons, just in the case the computer went down and you had to do things the old-fashioned way and press a button.

"Engines look a-okay," Zenna said.

"We are cleared for near hyper-speed. Searcher 0.5 is currently in orbit 1000 kilometers above Mars. I've laid in a course," Elvin said. "The computer had one laid out, but mine actually saves us seven tics. I estimate the flight to be six minutes and twelve tics."

"Could you be more exact?" I asked, jokingly.

"I could, but it would be wasted on you," Elvin said, seriously.

I positioned myself a little better into the pilot's seat. It just felt right. "I'm locked and loaded," I said.

"Actually we only have tractor beams," SC-711 corrected from the ship's intercom.

"Figure of speech there, SC," I said.

"Oh, I knew that," SC-711 said.

GiS gave me "the look." "Don't give the computer a hard time," he said.

I nodded my agreement. This was not the time to pick an argument.

"We are cleared for departure," SC-711 said.

"We?" I asked.

"I will be functioning as your ship's computer interface for this mission," SC-711 said.

"I'm honored," I said.

"As well you should be."

The red lights in the bay area started to flash. A warning horn sounded. (This whole place was big on lights and sirens.) These meant the big bay doors were going to open in thirty seconds. It was time for all personnel to clear the surface. If you weren't in a shuttle, you shouldn't be there.

"The surface is clear," SC-711 said.

The big bay door our shuttle was facing slowly started to roll open. It only took maybe ten minutes, but it seemed like ten hours. There, lying before us was an infinite collection of stars. They were all calling my name. But for now I had to concentrate on the mission at hand.

"We are cleared for go," SC-711 said.

I looked at GiS. He nodded his head.

"Starting engine," I said.

I pressed the engine ignite button on the top left control panel. The shuttle's engine roared to life.

"Starting liftoff power," I said. I pressed the ignite button again.

We rose ever so slightly off the landing pad.

"Switching to forward power," I said. I moved my index finger and pressed the yellow accelerator button located right next to the start button. I pressed it gently. We wanted to ease out. Nice and slow.

The shuttle started to move forward toward the open door. My job here was simple, just to keep the shuttle straight.

"Easy, easy," GiS said nervously. "Don't be nervous," he said.

"No problem," I said as we glided closer and closer to the freedom of space.

"Don't be nervous," GiS repeated.

"I won't be nervous as long as you don't keep saying don't be nervous," I said.

GiS just looked at me with a raised eyebrow. It was a look only a chimp could give. I was sure he wanted to say, "It's my job to say that," but he fought the urge.

"You're doing fine," he said. "Just don't get cocky."

I steered the shuttle through the door. We were in space! The final frontier. (Even though oceanographers like to call the ocean the final frontier. But they're just jealous. After all space is infinite; oceans aren't.)

"Nice job," GiS said. "Now, stay focused."

I pressed the accelerate button in a bit more. We pulled away from the station. The station appeared on our rear view screen. As it was growing smaller and smaller I was pretty certain the smile on my face was growing wider and wider.

"Don't put it to near hyper-speed until we're 300 kilometers from the station." GiS said, though he knew I knew that.

"Don't worry," I said.

"It's one of my jobs to worry," he said.

"Then don't worry so much," I said.

He nodded. "I will do my best," he said. "Though it's not easy."

I peered out the side window. When possible, I preferred to use the windows instead of the view screens. The windows just seemed more natural. Kymm and her shuttle were running right beside us. She blew me a little mock kiss, at least she wanted to believe it was a mock. Yep, she liked me alright. At least I think she liked me. Maybe her mock kiss really was just a mock kiss?

"Keep your eyes and brain in the game," GiS coached.

I blocked Kymm from my mind for now. We had a mission. I needed to focus all my attention on that, for now.

"We are now 300 K from the station," Elvin said. "The course is plotted. We can now safely go to near hyper-speed."

I looked over at GiS. He nodded his approval. I pressed the accelerator button to launch us into near hyper-speed, NHS for short. The stars before us suddenly blurred into streaks of bright light that seemed to be coming toward us. They weren't, of course. We were actually zooming toward them at a speed that wasn't light speed but was pretty darn close. I pitched the ship a couple degrees to the right as we rocketed forward. I fought back the urge to yell whoopee! I was on a mission. Not just any mission, but one with the fate of two worlds at stake. No pressure there.

Chapter 9

I F I SAID I WASN'T TOTALLY ELATED piloting my shuttle through space I would be lying through my teeth. This was without a doubt the greatest moment of my life. Not only was I racing toward the stars, but I was on a mission — a real mission. I knew my face must have been one giant grin.

"Enjoying yourself, Scout?" GiS asked.

Something told me that there was no right answer to that question. My best shot was to come up with something that wouldn't upset GiS, but I wasn't sure that was possible.

"I have great anticipation," was all I said.

I adjusted the shuttle's control stick just a hair. I didn't really need to. With the computer course laid in, my only job as pilot was to keep us on course. I just wanted to look busy in the hopes that GiS wouldn't continue this line of questioning.

"Hey, why did you change the pitch .05 degrees?" Elvin asked, definitely not helping me out here. "That will slow our arrival down by five tics!"

"Yes, Baxter why did you do that?" GiS asked. I didn't take my eyes off the view screen, but I knew he had one eyebrow raised.

"Instinct," I said. "This course just feels better."

GiS just shook his head. "When on a pre-laid course, proper pilot procedural protocol is to simply follow the computer's lead and keep the ship steady."

I knew GiS was going to come back at me with proper pilot procedural protocol, or p-cubed as we young pilots called it. P-cubed was just an overly fancy way of saying let the computer do it. My guess was that if whoever it was that made up these rules could figure out a way to do this without humans, they would. The thing is, as good as computers are when it comes to repetitive processes, when things get dicey and the poop hits the solar-powered fan, computers still don't act as well as the best humans.

We have something they still haven't figured out how to program into computers. To be polite, I call it instinct but it's really something more. It's having the guts to do something that seems ridiculous but you know it's not. It's reacting to the problem that you know is going to follow the current problem. It's almost a sixth sense — a way of reacting out of the ordinary to something out of the ordinary. Whatever it is, it's something scientists haven't learned to break down into a mathematical formula, at least not yet. So for now there are still some things we do better than machines.

I didn't bother to look over at GiS but I knew he was shaking his head.

"Baxter," he said, surprisingly calmly, "you *do* have incredible reactions, it's a gift that not many have."

"Thanks," I said, taking whatever I could get.

"But…" GiS said.

With GiS there is always a but. In this case I knew it was going to be a big but.

"But," he repeated, "you have to learn the appropriate time to use that gift. You need to know when to act and when not to act."

"The adjustment just felt right," I said.

"Searcher 0.5 is coming into view now," Zenna announced, saving me from having to go any further with the conversation with GiS.

Sure enough, there on the screen growing larger and larger by the tic was Searcher 0.5; a giant, reflective metal sphere that could move people and equipment faster than light. It was an impressive sight and an impressive technological achievement. It wasn't as big as a space station, but it could still hold a dozen ships and à crew of up to two hundred organics, non-organics and mixes.

"We'll talk about this later," GiS said.

Not if I could help it, we wouldn't.

"Slow to approach speed," GiS ordered.

"Right," I said in my most business-like voice.

Elvin made a few adjustments at his panel. "I have the course laid in," he said.

"Just follow the computer's prompts," GiS reminded me.

Before I could acknowledge, Kymm's voice came over our intercom.

"Ah, New Houston, we have a problem," she said cautiously. I could tell she was scared but trying hard not to sound it.

"Why is she talking to Houston?" Zenna asked, not surprisingly not getting the reference.

"What's up, Kymm?" I asked, over the ship to ship intercom.

"Uh, we can't slow our ship down or change its course," she said. "The computer systems aren't responding!"

"What gives, SC-711?"

"It's not SC," Kymm said over the intercom. Though I couldn't see her, I could hear the sweat in her voice. She was struggling with all her might to slow her ship down.

"While I am acting as the master computer for the shuttles, each shuttle has 1,032 other computers onboard that dictate other functions. For instance there is a …"

"You're taking too much time here, SC!" I interrupted. "I don't need the whole story, just the main plot!"

Like I said earlier, there are some things computers just don't get. At least not yet. I'm not sure if they ever will. That's why I'm glad I don't have any chips wired into me.

"The other computers are ignoring my commands," SC said quickly.

"Well, that's not good," Elvin said.

For a bright guy Elvin had a way of stating the obvious.

"If I don't slow down or gain some control soon, I'm going to crash into Searcher! Nothing can help me land at this speed," Kymm said, as calmly as she could, considering the situation. She was good, I had to give her that.

"Can you move Searcher out of the way?" I asked SC.

"Yes," SC answered.

"Then do it!" I said.

"I can do it," SC said slowly. "Only with Searcher locked in orbit and prepared to accept boarding ships, it will take five minutes for me to move it."

"Why didn't you tell me that sooner?" I asked.

"You didn't ask," SC said.

"We don't have five minutes," I said.

"Hence the reason I never mentioned it," SC said.

"SC, what's the standard procedure for dealing with an out of control ship?" GiS asked, scratching his head with one hand and his butt with the other.

"We would be forced to use Searcher's laser cannons to destroy the offending ship," SC paused for a tic. "Of course the cannons are off line and would take five minutes to activate."

"Doesn't matter," I said. "I don't like that option anyhow."

"It doesn't matter if you like it or not," SC said coldly. "There is nothing I can do with either Searcher 0.5 or Shuttle K-II to keep the two from colliding."

"The crash will be devastating!" Elvin said, once again feeling obligated to point out the obvious.

"Yes," SC agreed. "At their speed and angle of approach, I estimate there is a 57.325 percent chance of the impending explosion also destroying the Searcher 0.5."

"Really?" Elvin said. "I estimate there is a 57.322 percent chance of them destroying the Searcher."

"Hmmm," SC said. "Perhaps you did not properly take into account mass of the ship now that Chriz and Lobi have each put on an additional kilo?"

"Missing the big picture here!" I shouted.

Elvin glared at me. "It's my job to track every little detail!"

"Track," I said. Something about that word sparked a chain reaction in my mind.

I thought for a tic more. "Elvin, you're brilliant."

"I know that," he said confidently, even though he had no idea where I was going with this. "Why do you know that?"

I turned to Zenna. "Zen, give me tractor beams, full power!"

"Right!" she said excitedly. She knew where I was going with this.

So did GiS.

"Baxter you can't grab a shuttle moving at a near light speed with a tractor beam! It's a nearly impossible shot."

"Not impossible, but nearly a million to one," Elvin corrected.

"They just need to cut their engines," I said.

"Baxter, I know you like to sleep in physics class, but even Zenna knows even if they cut their engines they wouldn't just stop! The centrifugal force would still carry them forward."

Zenna nodded. "Yep, even I know that," she said proudly.

"Yes, but they will slow down!" I said.

Kymm and her crew had been listening to our conversation. "I hope you know what you're doing, Moon," she said. "Okay, I'm going to emergency manual override now. I've cut the power."

Elvin looked at his console. "They have slowed down .05 percent."

"That's a start," I said.

"Okay, SC, give me control of the ship now," I said.

"If you insist," SC said.

GiS looked at me. He looked at the view screen with the Searcher growing larger and larger by the tic. He looked back at me. "Baxter, even if this works, you'll never stop it in time," he said. "They'll just pull us crashing into the Searcher also."

I hated to admit it but GiS was right. I couldn't stop the shuttles. But luckily I didn't have to stop them, at least not yet. I just had to nudge them past Searcher, then stop them.

"How long until impact?"

"Two minutes and thirty seconds," Elvin and Lobi both said.

"Plenty of time!"

I turned to Zenna. She was one step ahead of me. She was already under her console making the needed adjustments.

"One electronic pool cue coming up," she said.

"What are you guys talking about?" Kymm asked over the intercom.

"I'm going to use the tractor beam as a pool stick and I'm going to bounce you guys over the Searcher, then I'll catch you and tow you back in."

There was dead silence from the other ship.

"This is doable," I said.

We heard a big sigh over the intercom.

"I can do this," I said.

"I've seen you play pool," Kymm said.

'Trust me," I said.

"It's ready!" Zenna shouted.

"Trust me," I repeated.

"Do I have any choice?" Kymm said.

I was determined to let my actions be my answer. "Give me a laser sighting," I said.

An electronic circle appeared on the view screen.

"Do you wish me to take the shot?" SC said in his calm computer voice.

"No," I said firmly. We had had enough problems with computers these last two days. If this was going to work I was going to have to do it myself. "I'll use the left control stick as tractor control."

I was surprised that GiS didn't complain or make any suggestions. It was out of character for him. I figured he either trusted me or had absolutely no faith that this idea would work.

"Slow to impulse power," I ordered.

"Check," Elvin said.

I felt the ship slow down. The stars and Searcher were still coming toward us, but not as fast. I lined up the cursor with the back end of Kymm's shuttle. I held my breath. I adjusted the cursor just a tad. Don't know why I did. It just felt right. I had to aim and time this perfectly. Well, at least as perfectly as a human could. I pulled the trigger. I took a breath. All I could do now was watch and hope.

I focused on the view screen. Sure enough, Kymm's shuttle had started to pitch upward. I had hit it. Now the question was did I hit it right? Was I able to deflect it over the Searcher?

We all held our collective breath as Kymm's shuttle rose higher and higher while at the same time moving closer and closer to the Searcher. It was going to be close, really close. The shuttle passed over the top of the Searcher. It caused a few sparks when it clipped the top ever so slightly, but that was it. We had done it. We saw it plain as day in the view screen as Kymm's shuttle passed mostly harmlessly overhead.

"We did it!" Zenna shouted.

"Turn!" GiS shouted. "Turn."

Sure enough Searcher was growing ever larger in our view screen, which meant we were getting ever closer. In fact the Searcher now filled our view screen. Which meant we were way too close.

"I'm turning! I'm turning!" I shouted back.

I jammed the control stick to the right. The ship rolled to the right so hard I thought I was going to put us into a tail spin, but somehow I managed to keep us from flipping. I had to keep her steady now until we shot past Searcher. We were probably close enough to Searcher to reach out and touch it, but the important thing was we weren't touching it. The force exerted on my ship was incredible, but I knew I had to keep her straight.

"Tell me when we have cleared Searcher," I yelled.

"I will," Elvin yelled back. There was silence. There was more silence. Still more silence. Finally Elvin yelled, "We're clear!"

"You know, there's no need to yell, you two," Zenna noted. "You're both less than three meters from each other."

"Good point, sis."

"Sorry, just got lost in the moment," I said, while holding the control stick firmly to keep the shuttle straight, but gently enough to be able to respond to anything that might pop up.

I took a deep breath. I slowed to sub-impulse speed. I took another deep breath.

"Nice job, team," GiS said. "But before you get too cocky, remember that all we really accomplished was to not kill ourselves or blow up our ship within the first hour of our mission. In fact, our problems have now put us fifteen minutes behind schedule."

"Fifteen minutes and twenty two tics," Elvin corrected.

"All the more reason to regroup and prepare," GiS said.

Part of me felt like telling GiS off. We had done more than that, I thought, but thinking a bit more, I knew he was right. All we really succeeded in doing was not ending our mission before it started.

"Where's Kymm's shuttle?" I asked.

"I was able to get reverse thrusters online so they have come to a complete stop. They are in section 23.7 of this quadrant. They are a mere 1001 kilometers away," SC answered.

"Actually it's 1001...," Elvin started to say.

"Actually, Elvin that super exactness gets old really fast," I said.

"Agreed," SC said.

"I'm forced to agree with Baxter, Elvin. There are times when we need to be exact, but we don't need to be exactly exact all the time," GiS stated.

"It's about time you guys told him that!" Zenna chimed in. "It's not like this is rocket science." She stopped to think about what she said for a few tics. "Okay, maybe it is rocket science, but it's still annoying."

GiS and I nodded our heads in agreement.

Elvin shrank back a bit. "Sorry, sometimes I may get a nano, quantum, wee bit carried away."

"No problem," I said.

Kymm's voice came booming over the intercom. "While I hate to break up your little love fest, my shuttle is dead in the water here and I'm going to need a tow into dock."

I looked up at the intercom.

"Right, Kymm, I'll be right there."

"What does she mean by, dead in the water? We're in space." Zenna said.

"Figure of speech, Zen," I said.

Zenna smiled. "Oh right, I knew that!"

Chapter 10

Aour tractor beam to tow Shuttle K-II into the Searcher. I had
towed shuttles in simulators at least a hundred times. The last
ninety of them I had done it flawlessly. Even though this wasn't
a simulation, the simulators were surprisingly accurate, so I was
prepared. Towing is actually an easy procedure. Just latch on
to the ship with your tractor beam, stay 100 meters behind the
ship and 30 degrees above it as you guide it to its destination
and then gently push it in. Then, after the landing bots roll it
out of the way, you drop down to landing level and then land
yourself. Easy as pie, or in Elvin's case, pi. That's what I kept
telling myself.

The only problem was my nerves. We had locked on to
Kymm's shuttle easily enough. Towing it to the sphere wasn't
much harder. We were in gravityless space. The weight of the
shuttle we had locked our tractor beam on made little difference
in the handling of my shuttle. I just had to remember that there
was another shuttle being pulled in front of us that I had to
guide into the docking bay. Whenever my nerves would kick in,

telling me this wasn't a simulation and if I mess up we're dead, I would imagine I was still on the simulator. I know it seems lame but it worked for me. (Once I tried picturing Commander Jasmine in a bikini, but that didn't turn out well at all.)

The landing bay door on the base of the sphere opened once we were within a kilometer of the Searcher. The Searcher, while not being a floating city in the sky like our base, was still quite large, the size of a big hotel. After all, it was meant to house a couple of hundred beings on long-term missions. The landing bay also wasn't as super humongous as the one on the base but it was still large enough to house at least a dozen shuttles.

"Ease her in carefully," GiS said, using his best mentor voice.

I fought back the urge to say, no kidding.

"When the towed shuttle is within 100 meters of the bay, cut all engines, activate the stabilizers, then slowly push her in."

"No kidding," I said, failing this time to fight back the urge.

"I know you know this," GiS said, a bit testy. "I'm just reinforcing it. It's my job to make sure you do your job right."

"I'll tell you when Shuttle K-II is within 100 meters of the Sphere," Elvin said. He looked at his console and started counting down. As he counted down I lined up our shuttle with the door.

"500 meters, 400 meters, 300 meters, 200 meters, 100 meters."

I cut our engines and hit the stabilize button. The ship rocked a bit and then came to stop. I could see into the landing bay through the view window. The other shuttles were lined up perfectly.

Elvin looked at his console. "Kymm's shuttle is 2 degrees off center to the right of the optimal landing spot," he said.

Okay maybe it wasn't perfect, but it was good enough.

I looked at the intercom. "Are you ready, Kymm?"

"As I'll ever be," she responded. "This is easy, Moon, just guide us in and let us go."

"You can do it, Bax old buddy," Chriz said, apparently for once in his life not wanting to tick me off.

"I didn't think you liked Baxter," Lobi said, apparently forgetting that we were in communication over the intercom.

"Ssh, you fool," Chriz said.

"Quiet both of you," K-999 ordered. "Scout Moon needs to concentrate."

I decreased the power of the tractor beam. Their ship started to pull away from us toward the Sphere. As I continued to slowly cut the power of the tractor beam their shuttle moved closer and closer.

"We're in," Kymm said.

Elvin looked at his console. "My readings confirm that," he said, apparently not trusting Kymm's eyes, bionic or not.

I cut the tractor beam power. Through the view screen I could see Kymm's shuttle drop to the floor like a big expensive brick.

"Are you guys alright?" I asked through the intercom.

"We're alive," Kymm said. "It could have been softer, but we'll walk away and like they say..."

"Any landing you walk away from is a good one," I said completing the sentence for her.

"Who's they?" Zenna asked.

"The landing bots will have them moved out of the way in 300 tics," SC informed us.

I pushed the handle down just enough to drop our shuttle into line with the bay door and waited. For once in my life I didn't mind waiting. It gave me a chance to catch my breath and wipe the sweat from my hands.

I turned and looked at my squad.

"We did it," I said.

Elvin and Zenna both smiled. GiS pointed forward to the bay door.

"They are ready for you to land now," he said.

"That is correct," SC confirmed.

"Then let's bring her in," I said.

I turned off the stabilizers and nudged the control stick forward. We were so close to the Searcher I didn't need much power. I just floated her in.

I turned off my shuttle and looked around. I couldn't help smiling. I had towed one shuttle and landed my shuttle on a real warp-capable Searcher-class space sphere. We had been on simulator versions of Searcher before, but this was the real thing. Now there would be no imagining I was on a simulator. I wanted to soak it in all in. I deserved it.

GiS must have seen the look on my face. "Wipe that silly grin off your face, Scout Moon," he ordered. "We've just started this mission and we're already behind schedule, and we may be one shuttle down. To make matters worse we have no idea what went wrong with that shuttle."

I released my flight harness and stood up. I wanted to tell GiS to lighten up. He always had a way of finding the worst in any situation. The thing is, in this case he was right and I knew it. Last week I probably would have argued for the sake of arguing, but not today. This wasn't the time. We had a mission to accomplish. This was my first real mission and I was determined to make it a success. Even if that meant not arguing with GiS.

"You're right, again, Commander," I said, hanging my head just a bit.

GiS unbuckled his harness and then just stood there. He was dumbfounded. He wasn't expecting to me to agree that easily. It threw him off stride. He adjusted his uniform and straightened up.

"Of course I'm right," he said.

He patted me on the shoulder with his foot.

"You did good, Baxter."

"Thanks," I said.

"Of course with all the time I've spent training you, you better do good," he added, though I swore he wasn't quite as dead-on serious as he usually was when he said these things. "Now come on, we've got a job to do!"

He walked off the shuttle.

I looked at Elvin and Zenna. I shrugged.

They shrugged.

We followed GiS out of the shuttle on to the deck of the Searcher's landing bay. You know how they say if you've been in one landing bay you've been on them all? Well, that doesn't hold true when you are on a warp-class Sphere's landing bay. Though it looked like a smaller version of the space station's landing bay — a big open area surrounded by launch door — the thing was, knowing that this landing bay was inside a sphere that could go faster than light and travel to other galaxies made it special.

We had all been on simulated Spheres before, but none of us, not even GiS, had ever been on a real one.

"Zap!" Elvin exclaimed. "We're on a real intergalactic faster-than-light sphere!" he said, echoing my thoughts.

GiS looked around unimpressed. "No big deal. We've done this simulation module enough so you should all feel right at home."

I just looked at him.

"Okay, maybe not right at home," he admitted. "But close enough to get the job done."

We walked over to the exit elevator door where we were met by Kymm and her team. They looked a little shook up, but not much worse for the wear. It's not like Lobi and Chriz were that much to look at even when they were at their best.

Kymm extended her hand to me. "Nice work, Moon," she said, "though I would have done the same for you, only with a smoother landing."

"A much smoother landing," Chriz added.

Kymm shot him a look. He sulked back. Yep, she had a thing for me alright.

I shook Kymm's hand. All I said was, "You're welcome."

"Do you think what caused the malfunction on our shuttle could be related to what happened to Axel?" K-999 asked GiS.

GiS rubbed his chin with his foot. "I don't like to speculate," he said.

"Then just guess," Zenna said.

"I'd guess yes," I said.

GiS looked at me. "It's still too early to know." He looked at his watch. "It's 0900 now; report to your quarters. We'll meet in the conference room at 0930 to discuss options."

"That's in thirty minutes," Zenna whispered to me.

"Thanks, I figured that out," I told her.

We all stepped on to the elevator.

"SC-711, what floor are we staying on?" K-999 asked.

"I have assigned you all adjacent rooms on level 13."

"Now, that's an omen if ever I heard one," I mumbled.

"Will we have single rooms?" Kymm asked as the elevator started to rise.

"Yes," SC answered. "The rooms here are much smaller than your quarters but they are single occupancy. This sphere has room for up to two hundred crew and a hundred passengers, and since there are only eight of you, I thought it was logical to dedicate a floor to you."

"Good computing," I told SC.

I personally was thrilled to have a room to myself. It probably stems from me being an only child back at home. I respect my crew and I'm use to having them around me all the time, but there are times when it would be great to have my own space. I looked at Zenna. She had that look about her, a cross between her trying to think and being worried.

"What's wrong, Zen?" I asked.

She looked down and lowered her eyes. "Uh, nothing."

Then it hit me. Zenna, being a twin, probably had never had a room to herself. She was scared. Bloop, I had never seen Zenna scared before. I've seen her confused many times. I've seen her baffled. I've seen her confused and baffled, just never scared.

"Don't worry, Zen, it will be okay."

Zenna looked up at me. "It's just that..."

"All the rooms are connected," SC said, being surprisingly helpful. "Your brother Elvin will be in the room to your right and Baxter will be in the room to your left."

Zenna thought about it for a tic. "Well," she said slowly, "with having a room to myself, at least I don't have to worry about my foot odor accidentally knocking anybody out."

"See, that's a plus for all of us," I said.

Zenna forced a smile, I knew she was trying to convince herself. "It probably won't be too bad."

"Of course it won't be. Bloop, Zen, you're stronger than all of us put together."

"I know that," she told me, speaking as if I was denser than the core of a white dwarf star. "I just don't want to be lonely."

"Your room has doors that open to your brother's and Baxter's room," SC added.

Zenna looked at Elvin. "Will you keep your door open?"

"Sure, Sis," he said.

Zenna looked at me. "Will you leave your door open?" she asked.

"I won't lock it," I offered.

Zenna looked at me with big puppy dog eyes.

"Fine, I'll leave it open a little," I sighed.

"Great!" she said.

Kymm leaned over to me. "Nice just easing the fears of a teammate," she whispered. I wasn't sure if she was being cynical or not. I decided to believe she wasn't.

"You guys are the best!" Zenna said.

Almost on Zenna's remark the elevator stopped. The doors opened.

"We have reached the 13th level. Please proceed out of the elevator to the right," SC said, acting like an electronic tour guide.

We followed SC's instruction and entered the hallway. There wasn't much to it, it was just a hallway. I imagine hallways haven't changed much in the last couple hundred years, just walls dotted with doors and cheap lights. The only thing special about this hallway is that it happened to be on a sphere that goes faster than light, which in my humble opinion made it pretty sweet.

As we walked, GiS talked, well, more like lectured. "We have no time to waste. SC, how long before the warp engines are ready?"

"I am charging them now. They will be ready for warp burst in one hour and forty-two minutes and thirteen tics."

"Very good," GiS said.

That's the thing about warp burst engines, while they are way fast, they take a while to prepare. I'm not entirely sure about the physics involved (though I am sure Elvin, Chriz or Lobi would be all to happy to explain them to me) but I do know it consists of mixing matter and antimatter to create worm pathways in space. These pathways are cosmic short cuts from one place to other.

The other problem with warp burst engines is they are energy hogs. Once you warp burst to someplace you are dead in the water for a good deal of time. This means warp burst equipped spheres are great to hop from place to place if you plan to stay there and look around for a while. It makes the Searcher-class ships great research ships but lousy war ships. Which most of the time is fine as Searchers are exactly that — searchers. It is their mission to explore and to search out new life and all that jazz. We don't want them warp bursting around the universe shooting things up. That's not the way to make friends.

Of course we're not stupid either. We know that certain parts of the universe may not be as friendly and as open to us as we would like them to be. Some parts may even be downright hostile. I remember a class on possible alien cultures once where my professor had a theory that there might possibly be races out there that are so appalled by the way we smell they would want to destroy us. Luckily we haven't run into any race like that. And quite frankly, to me any race that has evolved to the point of intergalactic space travel and has the capacity to destroy us would probably be smart enough to develop air filters so we wouldn't offend them so much. Or at the very least hold their breath when they are around us. Still, since the possibility of hostile encounters certainly exists, we don't go into these missions blindly. Searchers do come equipped with laser cannon batteries in all directions. We may come in peace, but we don't want to leave in pieces. Searchers obviously don't pack the pure power of the missile-loaded battle cruises, but they are capable of defending themselves.

In this case, though, we were heading into potentially hostile territory with our weapons off-line. We'd be motionless and defenseless. I decided it was better not to think about it.

I went into my room and looked around. It was your basic room, bed, desk, closet, computer screen with a small bathroom on the side. It was Spartan but it served its purpose. Plus, it was mine, just mine.

I sat down on the bed, just to test its mattress. I was pretty certain that Earth Force regulations required a firm mattress. I was right, the mattress recessed just enough to give in to my weight, no more. It certainly wouldn't be like sleeping on air. But I was sure GiS would say we are not here to sleep.

There was a knock at the bottom of my door. It was like somebody was banging the door with their foot.

"Come in," I said.

The door receded into the wall. A little meter-tall bot that looked like a box on wheels, was in the doorway.

"Greetings, Scout Moon. I am personal assistant bot PA-2407," the bot squeaked in a high pitched sound that matched its diminutive size. "Are you in need of any toiletries? "

I just looked at the bot. Being a cadet I wasn't use to having a bot actually wait on me. Sometimes I think our commanders think cadets are lower on the food chain than bots.

"You know toiletries: soaps, shampoos, shaving cream, a shaving laser?" the bot said, almost as if it was apologizing.

"I know what toiletries are," I said.

"I'm sorry," the bot said, more apologetically, rolling backwards. "It's just the last cadet I asked, told me and I quote: 'No thanks, I have a toilet in the room.'"

"That must have been Zenna," I said.

The bot rolled forward again. "Yes sir, I believe it was. My sensors detected she was female. Once I explained to her what toiletries were, she requested two vials of anti-foot-odor nano-bots."

"Yep, definitely Zenna," I said.

The bot rolled into the room. A couple of telescoping robot arms and hands folded out of the bot's sides. Each arm reached into the bot's storage area. The bot pulled out some shaving cream and a shaving laser.

"I will leave you additional shaving cream and shaving laser," it said.

"I only shave twice a week."

"Yes, in real space, but things work differently when warp bursting. As far as my data banks show, you and your crew will be the first adolescents into true hyperspace. Who knows how your bodies will react?" it said. "You humans may play with the time-space continuum but you still do not understand it. It never hurts to look nice," the bot concluded.

I wasn't going to argue. I didn't have a leg to stand on. Was the bot correct? Would we be the first teens to travel faster than light? I thought for a tic. He probably was right. Wow, I had never thought of that. Our mission was going to be even more significant than I thought.

The bot rolled out of the room. I was pretty sure it said, "Have a nice warp. If you need me just send me an email," but truthfully, I wasn't paying a lot of attention. I was deep in thought, at least as deep in thought as I ever get. Were we really going to be the first teens in hyperspace? Did they know how that might affect us? Did they care? What the bloop were we doing out here anyhow? We're just a bunch of kids. Sure we've been training for a few years, but we have no experience.

I couldn't help thinking that maybe Earth Gov wanted us to fail. Did they maybe they want a war? Maybe they thought the planet was getting too complacent and a war would shock us into working harder. Maybe they thought ten billion people on the planet were too many. Did they want to cull some out? Maybe I was just thinking too much? Maybe I had read too many conspiracy blogs.

Before I got too deep into my thoughts, SC came on over the intercom.

"As per GiS's request, I have loaded all mission data into your quarter's personal computer station," SC said.

"Thanks," I said, leaving the world of the paranoid.

"I have also downloaded all the specs from your shuttle and Shuttle K-II."

"Thanks," I said. Though I was pretty certain I wasn't going to look at those at all. I looked up at the screen. "What about transmissions to the shuttles?" I asked.

There was silence for a few tics. "I never computed the pos-sibilities that those would be important," SC said. There was more silence. "Why would they be important?"

"Just a hunch," I said. "I admit I have no idea where it came from."

"I will look into it," SC said.

When I arrived at the conference room, the rest of the group was already sitting around a long metal table, each staring down at the table's built-in computer screens. GiS looked up at me.

"You're late," he said.

"SC, what time is it?" I asked.

"09:29.90," SC answered.

"Well, you're the last one here," GiS said,

"So I've noticed," I said as I slid to the one open chair between Zenna and Kymm.

I sat down. I patted Zenna on the back. I gave Kymm my best smile.

"What have I missed?" I asked.

"Do you mean missed now?" Zenna asked.

"Ah, yes," I answered.

"Not much. GiS and K-999 were just explaining to us the importance of being prompt."

"Gee, sorry I missed that," I said.

Zenna leaned over to me and whispered. "Don't worry. You've heard it about a thousand times!"

"Thanks, Zen," I whispered back.

GiS cleared his throat to get our attention. We all turned toward him.

"We need to figure out sooner than ASAP what happened to Kappa's shuttle and how to fix it," GiS said.

"Scans have shown the shuttle is physically fine," K-999 said as gruff as ever.

"So why not erase the software, then copy Shuttle Sigma-II's software over it," Chriz suggested. "The two shuttles are identical; it should be a snap."

Elvin and Lobi just looked at each other. It figures the two super brains couldn't figure out the easy solution.

"That will work," Elvin said.

Lobi just nodded in agreement.

"Good," GiS said. "One problem solved. Of course that still doesn't tell us what caused the problem and how we can prevent it from happening again."

"It has to be related to what happened to Axel," Kymm said, as sure of herself as ever.

"It doesn't have to be," GiS said, keeping Kymm from getting too sure of herself. "But I admit, it is a possibility."

Kymm smiled to herself and then at me.

"I suppose it is possible to reprogram an android and a shuttle," K-999 said. "Difficult but possible."

"I could do it," Elvin said.

"So could I," Lobi said.

"Me too," Chriz added.

Zenna shook her head. "I might be able to, but I wouldn't want to."

I looked at the nerd squad. "Knowing how to do it and being able to do it are two completely different things."

The three of them just sat there with empty looks on their faces.

"The shuttles are constantly guarded. Axel may not have been constantly guarded but he was a highly programmed, combat-ready android. It's not like you could just walk right up to him and say, 'gee, Axel bud, let me reprogram you.'"

"I admit it wouldn't be easy," Elvin said.

"But we're clever. We'd come up with something," Chriz said.

"Yeah," Lobi added.

Zenna shook her head. "I'm not that clever."

"SC, run a scan and identify all people, animal and machines that have had contact with Axel and the Shuttle K-II over the last two weeks."

"There are 213 matches to your search," SC said.

"That narrows it down," I said cynically.

"Not by much," Zenna told me.

"Any other anomalies?" K-999 asked SC.

"Actually, yes," SC answered. "On a tip from Baxter I did a scan of remote transmissions and I found something strange.

Both Axel and the shuttle received an incoming transmission right before they went wacko."

Everybody at the table except for me and possibly Zenna looked surprised. I wasn't sure if they were more surprised by SC's statement or the fact that I was the one that pointed him in the right direction.

"Interesting," GiS said.

"Remote reprogramming," Elvin said.

"Very clever," Lobi said.

"Yeah," Chriz added.

"Here is what makes it very interesting," SC said. "The transmissions were carried on old television waves."

"The TVTrons!" Elvin, Zenna, Chriz and Lobi all concluded out loud at once.

"It does appear that way," GiS said cautiously. "But why?"

"Maybe they want a bigger audience?" I suggested.

"Whatever the reason, we need to inform Earth immediately," K-999 growled.

We all nodded in agreement.

"I'm afraid that will not be so easy," SC said. "All of our transmissions are being jammed."

"By the TVTrons?" GiS asked.

"By Earth Gov," SC answered.

"Why?" GiS asked.

"They do not want any of this to leak to the public. You know how the press is constantly trying to pick up and listen in on their transmissions. They figure the safest way to prevent that from happening is to prevent us from sending any back."

"But that doesn't make sense!" K-999 barked.

"I do not make the decisions. I just carry them out," SC said.

"Why weren't we told?" GiS asked.

"Apparently they did not think it would matter," SC said. "From what I deduce about chain of command, they give the orders and you all follow them." There was a slight pause. "Except occasionally for Baxter, he does not seem to be as eager to please as the rest of you."

"I just interpret the orders more loosely than others," I said.

"Perhaps that is why the commander chose Baxter. He thinks outside the cube," SC deduced. "Way outside the cube."

"Bloop, sometimes you can't even see the cube from where he thinks," Chriz said.

"Exactly," SC agreed.

Kymm laughed. I chose to take it as a compliment.

"Whatever the case, we are on our own," GiS said. He took a deep breath. He stood there in thought scratching his butt. He always scratched his butt when he was thinking hard. It was a weird habit, but he was an officer so nobody would ever tell him that.

"The warp engines are powering up. We should be ready in thirty-seven minutes," SC said.

"Good," GiS said. "Chriz and Zenna, you are in charge of reprogramming the Kappa shuttle."

"Right!" they both said.

GiS looked at Elvin and Lobi. "Elvin, Lobi, it's up to you two to find some sort of defense for our ships to prevent them from being reprogrammed by anybody else."

"Right!" Lobi said with a salute.

"Easy as grade school calculus," Elvin said.

"K-999 and I will work with SC to plot the safest warp course," GiS said.

"What about Baxter and me?" Kymm asked.

"Rest and stay loose," GiS said. "When the slop hits the propeller you two are going to have to be as sharp as possible."

While the others worked at their assigned tasks, Kymm and I walked around the sphere. Just soaking it in and talking. It certainly was an amazing machine and I was with a pretty girl, so it should have been the time of my life. Problem was, my mind was racing so I didn't enjoy the experience as much as I could have.

"What's wrong, Moon? You look more dazed than normal," Kymm said, poking me in the ribs, as we walked into the observatory at the top of the Searcher.

The walls of the room and the ceiling were transparent so no matter where you looked, you could see space all around you. There were no chairs but the walls were circled by a black metal bar that you could lean on. I walked over to the bar and looked out the window. Bloop, it was a great sight I should have been enjoying more, but I wasn't.

"I'm worried, Kymm."

"You'd be even crazier than I think you are if you weren't a little worried, Moon, I mean, Baxter. It's our first mission. Bloop, we're heading off into another galaxy in a ship that travels faster than light to try to prevent a war. We have the fate of two planets on our shoulders."

I turned my gaze from the stars to her. "That's the thing. Maybe they don't want us to succeed."

"Who?"

"Earth Gov. Maybe they want a war. Not an all-out war, just a little one."

"There hasn't been a war in decades."

"Exactly. Maybe they think a war will be good for us. Wake the populace up a bit. Plus it gives them a chance to test out all their latest weapons."

Kymm just looked at me. "You're crazy. At least I hope you are."

"I hope I am too."

Chapter 11

GiS CALLED US TO THE COMMAND CENTER in the center of the sphere. The bridge was a big impressive place. The room was meant to be manned by dozens of people and machines. It looked like a ghost room with just GiS, K-999, Zenna and Chriz in it. GiS and K-999 were sitting in command chairs in the middle of the room. Chriz and Zenna were watching the monitors and displays that lined the walls. For once I wasn't the last one to the meeting as Elvin and Lobi weren't there yet.

"We can't delay any longer," GiS said. "We must warp into hyperspace."

Just then almost on cue Elvin and Lobi came rushing into the control center. They were both covered with sweat and out of breath.

"Stop the sphere!" Elvin yelled dramatically.

"The sphere isn't moving yet," K-999 barked.

"Oh good," Lobi said.

"I assume you have something for us," GiS said.

Both Elvin and Lobi looked proud of themselves; their excitement was almost bursting out through their skin. They each wanted to talk first only they were getting choked up and tongue-tied with the urge to beat the other one to the announcement.

"Speak!" K-999 barked.

The two stood there, neither one able to say a word. They were smart dudes, but I could see why Kymm and I were the pilots.

Luckily SC spoke for them. "They have come up with a device that should screen any signals coming in and block out ones that have encoded messages aimed at our computers."

"Good," GiS said. "How long will it take to install?"

"It is downloading now," SC said. "I should have it online in three tics."

There was a pause.

"It is online now," SC said.

"We would have come up with it sooner, but we're not as familiar with the labs here as we are on the station," Lobi said.

"Good point," Elvin said, looking at Lobi.

They shook hands.

I turned to Kymm and whispered, "Could they be any geekier?"

"Nope, but we're lucky we have them."

GiS and K-999 were now all business. Not that they were usually loose, flexible, fun-loving commanders, but now they were more serious than I had ever seen them. You knew that they were really into this. This is what they were created to do — literally.

GiS looked up at the intercom like I like to do when talking to SC. "Are we ready for light speed, SC-711?" he asked.

"Yes, I said that earlier," SC said.

"Just making sure," GiS said, a bit defensively.

GiS pointed dramatically to the huge view screen on front of the wall.

"Take us out!" he said.

We all watched the screen. Instantly the stars that were filling the screen turned to bent streaks of lights; a dark black hole formed in the middle of all those bent streaks. It was like the hole had ripped apart a piece of the galaxy and that the galaxy was imploding into that rip. The hole pulled the light into it. We moved closer and closer to that hole until it engulfed the entire screen. Almost instantly everything reversed, The stars became black streaks and the space between them turned white. That meant we were inside this rip in space. We were in anti-space or hyperspace as the old TV shows liked to call it. The entire screen filled with crackling energy that looked like black bolts of twisted lightning. This was it, faster than light speed. We were moving over 186,000 miles per second but it didn't feel like we were moving at all.

"The jump will take ten minutes and twenty tics," SC said.

Einstein and other smart guys like him always said that *nothing can ever travel faster than the speed of light* and they were right. Okay, now you smart people are probably thinking, *if nothing can travel faster than light then how are you traveling faster than the speed of light*? The catch is that those smart guys needed to clarify that statement by saying nothing can ever travel faster than the speed of light in *our universe*. They missed the loophole that there is an anti-universe where everything travels faster than light.

Searcher-class spheres are able to create warp holes from one part of space that lead to another part of space. In a way they create short cuts through anti-space that allows moving from point A in regular space to point B in regular space very quickly. Think of where you start from as a dot on piece of paper. Think of your destination as a dot on the other end of the paper. When the paper was nice and straight the dots would be very far away for each other. Yet if you folded the paper in the middle the dots would move very close to other. That's what entering into anti-space gives us, a way to fold space together bringing the path to those to points closer together. I'm sure Elvin or Lobi and probably Chriz could give a long and very detailed explanation of what anti-space is, but that would be mega boring. All you need to understand is that it's a great short cut.

"This is cool," Kymm said to me, nudging me a little.

"Wow, the real thing is even better than the simulator," Elvin said.

We were all looking up at the screen in awe. This was mega cool, almost subabsolute zero.

I turned to GiS. For a tic I thought I caught him smiling, or at least starting to break a smile.

"How long since you've traveled at hyper-speed?" I asked.

"Four years, thirteen days and a few hours," he said, sounding much more like Elvin than I was comfortable with. "I was one of the early flight testers of the two-man cruisers" he said proudly.

"Oh, I see," I said, with a raised eyebrow. "That would explain a lot of things."

GiS crossed his arms and raised both eye brows. "Traveling through anti-space is perfectly safe."

"Yeah, as long as all the anti-anti-space nullifiers are working," I said.

"Well, of course," GiS said. He patted one of the consoles as if it were his pet. "You do have to trust the technology. Which I do."

"Uh oh," SC said.

For those of you who don't deal a lot with super computers, it's never a good sign when they uh oh.

"What's wrong?" K-999 barked. "I don't want anything to go wrong when we're in anti-space!"

SC paused for a tic which seemed like an hour. It's never good when the super computer needs to think so long about something. In fact it's pretty unnerving.

"Uh, SC." GiS coaxed. "What's wrong?"

"Actually, it is kind of funny," SC said.

For those of you who don't deal with super computers a lot, it's hardly ever funny when they say something is funny.

"Uh, what do you mean?" GiS asked

"My systems are under siege," SC said calmly. I had never heard the word siege used so casually before.

"That's not funny," Lobi said. "That's scary! How can you be so calm?"

Lobi was echoing most of our thoughts even though the rest of us wouldn't have sounded quite so panicked.

"I am programmed to always be calm," SC said, forgetting about the big picture.

"But we could die!" Lobi cried.

"Not we, you could die," SC corrected. "I am not technically or legally alive. Even if I were alive, this version of me is just a copy of my original system so even if this particular version of me were permanently deleted, other versions of me would live on."

"I still don't see why any of this is funny," I said.

"It is funny because the attacks echo the attacks on the shuttle and Axel," SC said.

"I still don't see why that's funny," I said,

Both crews nodded in agreement with me. It felt good to have everybody agree with me.

"Perhaps funny was not the best choice of words?" SC said. "Perhaps peculiar or unusual would have been better."

"Perhaps," I said, trying to get SC to offer up more info.

"Are we in danger?" Zenna shouted.

There was silence for a couple of tics.

"No, the updates to my software that Elvin and Lobi added alerted me to the problem. I was able to deflect the attacks."

We all breathed a sigh of relief.

"The good news is we are safe," GiS said.

"The bad news is, somebody knows we are coming," K-999 added, even though he didn't need to.

"Now this is where it gets funny," SC said. "The attacks were ordering me to turn off my weapon systems."

"But our weapon systems are already turned off," Zenna said.

"Exactly," everybody else said,

"Oh," Zenna said.

"So all they know about us is that we are coming," GiS said.

We all strongly suspected right there and then it had to be the TVTrons behind this. The question was, why?

Chapter 12

THE LAST FIVE MINUTES OF THE TRIP to Sirius D was about as uneventful a trip for the first teens in anti-space could be. We were all excited and any of us who said they weren't nervous would be lying. Bloop, it's only natural to be nervous on your first mission, and this was a big first mission. Nerves are good, they keep you alert and from getting too cocky. The trick is not to let them overwhelm you to the point of inactivity. It was a fine line, you wanted to be nervous but not afraid.

As we ripped through anti-space I found myself wondering what the bloop we had gotten ourselves into. Apparently the silent data attack on the Searcher had gotten to me more than I would have liked to admit. I like enemies that I see and touch. That way I feel I have some control of the situation. But an enemy that had the ability to remotely reprogram our machines to do their bidding meant they could hit us and we couldn't hit them back. Now that worried me.

Kymm elbowed me gently (well, gently for her) in the ribs. "What's up, Moon?" she asked.

"Nothing, just thinking."

"Ah," she said with a smile. "No wonder why you looked like you were pain."

"Ha, Ha. Very droll," I said. Yep, she liked me.

"If you ever leave the Scouts you have a career ahead of you as a stand-up comedian."

"At least I have a backup career," she said, elbowing me less gently.

I had to give the girl credit — she always had a comeback whether I wanted one or not. Just as I was about to give her a comeback to her comeback, SC interrupted.

"We will be leaving anti-space and arriving in the Sirius D system in thirty tics. I suggest you all be seated and harnessed in. Sometimes these returns to normal space can hit some turbulence."

We all sat down and buckled up. I focused on the view screen. We were still in anti-space but the area in front of us was getting narrower and narrower, almost closing in around us. It was like we were being rocketed through a tube that was constricting more and more by the tic. The entire sphere started to shake. I had been in a 5.9 earthquake once visiting my cousin in San Francisco. This shaking felt worse. It never felt like this in simulations. I held on to the chair. I didn't have to look at my knuckles to tell they were white.

"Uh, SC, this feels different," I said.

"Different from what?" SC said.

"Different from simulations," Kymm said.

"This is not a simulation." SC said. I'm not sure if he was trying to be reassuring, but he wasn't.

As the Searcher moved closer and closer toward the end of the anti-space tube, a veil seemed to separate the two universes. The closer we got, the more we rocked, and I don't mean rocked in a good way. Energy sparked all around us, crackling as if it was either mad at us or laughing at us. I fought the urge to close my eyes. If we were going break apart and die, I wanted to see it happen.

We hit the veil. The stars glowed white and the space between them was dark. The shaking had stopped. We were back in normal space. In the Sirius system. At least I assumed it was the Sirius system. It actually didn't look that different from our own galaxy. We were about 80 million miles from a bright yellow sun, roughly the size of our sun. We were between the second and third planets of the eight that circled that sun.

Actually it was kind of an anticlimax.

"So is this it?" Zenna asked.

There was a slight pause. "Yes, my readings confirm that this is the Sirius D system," SC said.

Elvin pushed a button. A console popped up in front of him. He ran his hands over the screen.

"Yes, I confirm SC's confirmation," Elvin said.

"Thank you," SC said, "though it wasn't needed."

GiS went into his mentor, I-am-smarter-than-you mode. He unbuckled his harness and stood up. He pointed to the screen.

"SC, please split the screen and show us a diagram of this solar system."

"No need to split the screen," SC said. "I will give you a holographic representation."

A mini-holographic sun appeared in the middle of the room. The sun was circled by two small planets, two earth size planets and four huge planets. There was a red dot flashing between the second and third planets, which I assumed was our position.

"This is the Sirius D solar system," GiS said, even though I was pretty certain we had known that.

"Oh!" said Zenna, you could almost see the light bulb go on inside her head. Okay, maybe we *all* hadn't gotten it.

"Currently we are located between the second and third of the eight planets in this solar system," GiS said. "They are both Earth-sized planets though neither of them is capable of supporting life, at least not life as we know it, as they each have extremely high concentrations of iron in their atmosphere and very strong magnetic fields. These strong magnetic fields create a sensor blocking zone between the two planets. That is why we are here, we should be invisible to any possible enemies looking for us while we scan for the Explorer."

Elvin and Lobi each raised their hands at the same time. GiS looked at them with a raised eyebrow. He knew they each had the same question. We all (except for maybe Zenna) had the same question. The rest of us just knew GiS would answer the question without us having to ask it. Deep down, Elvin and Lobi had to know this also, but they were so caught up in having to be the smartest they couldn't risk not asking, just on that slim chance that nobody else had thought of it.

"I know what you're thinking," GiS said cautiously. "That if these magnetic fields create a sensor blocking zone, how can we use our sensors?" he said.

Elvin and Lobi both lowered their arms, disappointedly frowning.

"Well, I will tell you," GiS said. "Our top scientists and computers have figured out a way to compensate for the high magnetic field, and therefore our sensors won't be affected. That gives us a distinct advantage."

The frowns on Elvin and Lobi's faces grew.

"Why weren't we informed of this?" Lobi asked. "We could have been of assistance."

"Because you are still cadets!" he said sternly. "No matter how smart you may be, Earth has other resources that are at least as smart as you are and have more experience. They are the ones who solved this problem. They are the best of the best. They are what you will be if you work hard and listen and don't let your giant egos get in the way."

Elvin and Lobi both drooped their heads. I almost felt sorry for them. For a couple of guys who were sure bright, they weren't smart enough to see that coming.

Before they could sulk for long, though, a warning started to blare. The control room's lights started to flash red. I don't know who thought of this procedure. I know it's meant to show danger is approaching, but bloop, you would think you'd want no excess noise and the best lighting possible when in danger.

"What's wrong, SC?" K-999 asked.

"My sensors have picked up incoming ships coming from around the third planet," SC said calmly.

"I guess our scientists weren't the only ones to figure out how to scan through the magnetic field," I said.

"Yes, apparently not," GiS sighed.

"I detect six shuttle-sized ships," SC said.

The holographic display showed six small dashes. They were on the opposite side of the third planet but getting closer to us.

"How do we know they are hostile?" Lobi asked.

"They have activated their weapon systems," SC said.

"Maybe they are just cautious?" Lobi said.

"They have fired upon us," SC said.

"Okay, I'll stop talking now," Lobi said, dropping his shoulders and holding his hands behind his back.

"What do you mean, they fired on us?" GiS said, "They are still half a planet away from us!"

"Apparently they have very good homing weapons," SC said. "You can see them on the screen now."

We all turned back to the view screen. Sure enough six balls of energy were screaming toward us. We all braced for impact. The balls hit. Nothing happened.

"Now that was anticlimactic, " I said.

GiS glared at me.

"It sure was," Kymm agreed. "The question is why?"

The lights flickered off, then back on again.

"Now that can't be a good sign," I said.

"It was another data attack," SC said calmly. "They were trying to get me to drop my computer defense systems. Which is kind of ironic since my computer defenses are always down as per our agreement with the Aquarians."

"You can read their attack?" Elvin asked.

"Yes," SC answered. "I have learned from the defenses you installed how to do that. Of course now I have good news and bad news."

There was a pause. Apparently SC wanted to be prompted.

"What's the good news?" I asked, being a bright side kind of guy.

"Even if our computer systems had been on I could have easily defended against that attack but that attack was many times more sophisticated than the attack in anti-space, so our foes seem to be learning."

"If that's the good news, then what's the bad?" Kymm asked.

"They are charging up a different sort of weapon. From the energy signatures they appear to be standard energy weapons. They are also closing in on us."

GiS was quick to react. "Fine — we will manually or animally man the sphere's laser cannons. K-999 and I will take cannon number 1. Baxter and Elvin will man cannon number 2. Kymm and Chriz will man cannon number 3. Zenna and Lobi will man cannon number 4.

"But I'm a girl," Zenna said.

"No matter! Just get to your posts stat!" K-999 shouted.

Elvin and I quickly moved to the lift to go to cannon number 2. I of course made it to the lift tics before Elvin did though it seemed like a lot longer while I was waiting. Finally he made it in.

"Which floor?" the lift computer asked.

"Weren't you listening?" I said.

"I am a lift computer. I don't listen in on command center conversations!"

"Laser cannon 2, stat!" Elvin said in his most business-like voice.

The lifted zoomed upward so fast I was glad I hadn't eaten in a few hours. The lift stopped before I even had a chance to say slow down — I don't want to be killed in a lift crash. The door opened to the laser cannon room turret. Actually, it wasn't much more than a transparent bubble on the top of the sphere above the observatory. It wasn't big, just enough space for a two-being crew. It probably looked like a zit on the top of the face that was the sphere but right now this zit and the three other zits like it on the sphere being manned by the others were all that were keeping us alive.

I moved in and strapped myself into the left gunner's chair. Elvin sat in the right. Each of the chairs controlled one of the two guns and rotated so you could manually follow and track your targets. We put the head sets on and flipped down the eye patch sight. The way the cannons worked was simple yet ingenious.

You would spin toward the target while looking at it, and to fire, you only needed to press either of the fire buttons located in both of the chair handles. Each cannon could cover half our zone. We each had to rely on the other not to miss.

I was certainly excited. It was so absolutely cool to be seeing action, live action. But I knew that this wasn't a game or a simulation. One slip up from me or Elvin and it wouldn't be game over, it would be life over. Not just for me, but for everybody onboard. I had to make sure that wasn't going to happen. No way I was going to die, before I got to give a girl a real kiss.

I glanced over at Elvin. If I was nervous, he had to be terrified. After all, I was a pilot. I was the thrill seeker. Elvin was meant to think about things, to plan things out. He wasn't used to having to make life and death decisions instantly.

"Are you going to be okay?" I asked him.

Elvin smiled. "Of course," he said.

I looked at him. He looked at me looking at him.

"Really, Bax, I can do this," he insisted.

"I know you can," I said. Though I'm not sure my face matched my words.

Elvin shook his head. "I know that look. You think I'm a prime spaz. This isn't like sports. I have good reactions."

I just looked at him.

"Remember that time in that test flight when we had an engine burnout?" he asked. "We had five tics to get the engine up before that piece of space debris collided with us. I rerouted the engine drivers in three tics. You don't think that took quick hands and a quicker mind?"

He was right. I had totally underestimated him. I wasn't the entire team here. We each had our strengths and weaknesses. That's what made us a team.

I patted him on the shoulder. "Let's blast these suckers!" I said.

"Besides," Elvin added. "These weapon systems are so mega-high-tech, you just look at your target and push a button. Even Lobi can do that," he said with a smile.

I hope so, I thought, because I knew if we were going to get out of this, we were all going to have to do our jobs. I took a deep breath.

"Boogies will be in firing range in thirty tics," SC said. "Good luck."

"SC, you're a computer. I wouldn't think you'd believe in luck," I said.

"Baxter, don't hassle the computer," GiS scolded over the intercom.

"May the odds be with you then," SC said. "Does that make you feel any better, Scout?"

Surprisingly, it kind of did. Only I didn't have much time to think about why that was so; six alien craft were now in visual range. They were long black, flat rectangles. They reminded me of flying remote controls, like the ones you see in museums and in great-grandparent's homes.

"These are robotic drones," SC said.

"Good, this way I won't feel guilty about blowing them up!" I said.

The remote drones opened fire. Their initial barrage of shots hit the midsection of the Searcher, but didn't appear to do much harm at all.

"Damage report," GiS called over the intercom.

"Damage minimal," SC replied. "The ships don't have a lot of fire power, but the damage will add up."

One of the attacking remotes burst into flames.

"Yahoo!" Kymm screamed over the intercom. "First kill is mine, Baxter!"

I certainly wasn't going to let Kymm have all the fun. I might not have had a bionic eye, but I had something chips can't give you, at least not yet, great instincts. In fact, I think the electronics might even muck up our instincts. I swiveled my seat to the left. There were two flying remotes bearing down on us. I was determined to take them both out. I pulled the trigger. My first shots flew between the two attackers.

"Bloop!" I shouted.

Suddenly the trailing flying remote, burst into flames.

"Gotcha!" Elvin said, pumping his fist. "You're trying to do too much, Bax. You've got to be organized, take one at a time."

The lead ship was still bearing down on us. Only it wasn't firing.

"They've figured out their energy weapons won't hurt us enough so they are going to ram us!" K-999 shouted.

"They're not ramming anybody," I said. "I'm way too young to die!"

I concentrated. I locked my eyes on the encroaching enemy ship. I let him draw closer. I wanted to make sure I took him out. I squeezed the trigger. The attacking ship burst into flames.

"The remaining ships are going to try to ram the Searcher's midsection," SC said. "Apparently they want to disable the ship but keep you humans alive."

"Probably to torture us," Elvin said.

"Gee, Elvin, thanks. Just what I needed to hear."

The bad news was that from our angle on top of the Searcher we had a hard time seeing and therefore aiming at the remaining attacking ships. The good news was our teammates didn't. The flying remotes aimed at the heart of the Searcher in a wedge formation. It looked as if their plan was for the three of them to all crash into our sphere at about the same spot. Apparently their logic was that a big enough explosion at the heart of Searcher would cripple it. The logic was correct, but their execution was flawed. The three remotes were flying so close together they made easy targets.

GiS and K-999 hit the lead remote with a perfectly placed stream of shots. Their aim was so good that they split the front remote in half. The exploding debris from the first ship collided with each of the wing ships, causing them to career away from the Searcher right before they too were destroyed in a fiery orange explosion.

"Wow," I said as the explosions lit up space.

We held our collective breath waiting to see if there would be a second round of attacks. We scanned the seeing area with our eyes, spinning this way and that way, while SC scanned the outside area.

"I don't see anything," I said.

"Same here," said Kymm. "And I'm looking over wide spectrum."

"Ditto," GiS said.

"Well, I see a lot of stars but no attacking ships," Zenna said.

"My sensors show no activity within 300,000 kilometers," SC said.

"It looks like we can stand down now," K-999 said.

"That was easy!" Lobi said, excitedly.

"Apparently the TVTrons aren't used to fighting people who can actual fire back," I said as I got out of my seat.

"Either that, or they are setting us up for something bigger," GiS said. "I want everybody on the bridge in thirty minutes."

Chapter 13

WHEN I ARRIVED ON THE BRIDGE, I wasn't surprised to see that I was last one there. I checked my sleeve communicator; I still had almost a minute to spare so GiS couldn't yell at me.

"As always, you're the last one here," GiS called over to me, from the scanning station where he and the others were gathered.

I decided not to point out that I was actually early. "Sorry," I said as I walked over to join my comrades.

GiS pulled his ankle up to check out his watch. I have no idea why he actually kept a watch on his ankle. It had to be a chimp thing. A way of showing off how flexible he was. He squinted at the watch. "Well, I guess for you, this would be considered early."

"Did I miss anything?"

Lobi rushed over to me. "Not much," he said, far too excitedly for me to believe that I hadn't missed anything. "Only that we discovered where the Explorer is!"

"You did?" I asked.

K-999 looked up from the scanner. "We might have found it. Maybe..."

"Well, that's not quite as exciting," I said. "I'm hoping we have something a bit more definitive."

GiS looked up at the ceiling. "SC, show Baxter our latest info."

"Of course," SC said.

Holographic images of the solar system we were in filled the room again. "This is still our current position," SC said.

A holographic image of Searcher appeared between the second and third planets.

"We have picked up the energy signature of what may be the Explorer here," SC said. A red O started to flash between the forth and fifth planets. "If this really is the Explorer, then it is 500,000 kilometers away."

"If?" I said.

"I can't be certain it's a true reading," SC said. "It might be a sensor decoy. A trap. Especially since it just popped up on the sensors ten minutes ago."

"Oh, that does seem a bit weird," I said.

"We can't rule out the possibility that TVTrons can manipulate our sensors," Kymm said.

"Though I don't think they can," Elvin said.

"You base that on what?" Kymm.

"My scientific intuition," Elvin said proudly.

"That doesn't make me feel any better," Kymm said.

"I agree with Elvin," Lobi said.

"Still doesn't make me feel better," Kymm said.

"Me neither," GiS said. "But we still need to check it out."

"Shall we power up the shuttles?" I asked.

GiS and K999 both shook their heads. "Not until we get to visual range," they both said in unison.

"Then what?" I asked.

"We'll play it by ear," GiS and K999 both said at once. It was kind of creeping me out.

"You guys should do parties," I said.

They both glared at me. I decided to back up. I've never been one to argue with the "play it by ear" technique of planning.

"SC, bring the Searcher within 10,000 kilometers of the Explorer," GiS ordered.

"We can not be certain that that reading is the Explorer," SC pointed out even though there was no need to.

"We know that, SC, but it's still our best option." GiS said with a small sigh, showing far more patience with SC than he did with me.

"Acknowledged," SC said. "Moving toward destination at sub-light speed. We should be within visual range, if there is something to see, in about twenty minutes."

I felt the Searcher start to move. Well, actually I didn't feel the ship move, but the stars on the view screen were moving so I knew we were.

After about ten minutes of traveling (which seemed to take ten hours) SC announced, "If that really is Explorer out there, we will be within visual range in ten, nine, eight, seven, six, five, four, three, two, one, now..."

Sometimes I worried about SC.

We all looked at the view screen. Sure enough, off in the distance was another floating sphere that looked a lot like the one we were on. Only this one was dead in the water. From the distance we were at it looked like a small, dead moon.

"Yep, that's the Explorer alright," K-999 said.

"SC, do you pick up any signs of activity?" GiS prompted.

"Scanning now," SC said.

From the looks of it, I would guess no. You didn't need SC's sensors to tell a dead ship when you saw one.

"Actually, yes," SC said.

Okay, so I was wrong. I'm a kid. I'm going to be wrong from time to time.

"I detect that the Explorer is functioning at .01 percent of power."

"That can barely be considered functioning," Chriz said.

"True, but I also detect a faint life sign. From the schematics I would say the life sign is coming from the medical cryogenics lab."

"You're saying somebody is in stasis on the ship?" Elvin said.

"I'm not saying it's true. I'm just saying it appears that way."

"It's a trap!" Kymm said.

GiS scratched his chin with his foot. "Perhaps," he said slowly. "But we can't take that chance. We have to check it out."

There was silence for a nano or two. K-999 looked up at SC. "Can we activate the Explorer?"

"Yes, I have their access codes," SC said.

"Good — then do it," GiS said.

"I can't," SC said.

"Why not?" GiS asked.

"We're too far away," Elvin and Lobi both said.

"Oh," GiS and K-999 said.

"True," SC said. "I need to be within 1,000 kilometers before I can transmit to the Explorer. Even then I may only be able to activate certain systems. It depends on the damage to the Explorer and its computer system."

"Can you override their system with your own?" Kymm asked.

"I could, but…"

"If the TVTrons have a backdoor virus on the system it would infect SC," Chriz said.

"Correct," SC said. "The only way to assure that doesn't happen is to…"

"Totally erase the old system and reload SC," Chriz answered.

"How long would that take?" GiS asked.

"I would estimate fourteen hours," SC said.

"The Explorer would be totally dead while the transfer was going on," I said. "Right?"

Elvin and Lobi just nodded.

"Okay, then that's our backup plan," GiS said.

"I agree," K-999. "I have a bad feeling about hanging around here for too long."

"So what's the primary plan then?" I asked, though I knew I shouldn't.

GiS put his arm around me. "We're going to fly over to Explorer and check her out."

"Oh," I said meekly. "Sorry I asked."

Chapter 14

M Y SQUAD, GiS AND I WERE in my shuttle flying toward the Explorer. While it was still way cool to be flying in space on an actual mission it wasn't quite as subzero cool as it was the first time. I don't know if it was because we were flying toward a potential trap or if I was just getting used to the idea of flying actual missions. Whatever the reason, I wasn't as thrilled as before. That didn't mean I wasn't just as determined, though, to get the job done.

I was anxious to get to the bottom of what that life sign was on the Explorer. Even it was trap I wanted to get it over with. This was one of those times where the anticipation and the lack of knowing what we were getting into was the hardest part of the mission.

"Don't worry Baxter, it will be all right," GiS said in his most calming tone. I had to give him credit for picking up on my tenseness. Either he was a lot more observant than I gave him credit for, or I was a lot worse at hiding my fears than I thought.

The Explorer was now clearly in our view screen. It was just sitting there dark and lifeless in space. It looked very uninviting.

"We are now within 3,000 kilometers of Explorer," SC said.

"Okay, Baxter, start slowing our approach now," GiS order.

I cut the forward thrusters. When you are flying in zero gravity you can't just jam on the brakes and instantly stop. To stop you basically need to slow down and then use reverse thrusters to neutralize your forward progress. I would let the ship coast for the next 2,000 kilometers, gradually using the stabilizers to bring her to a complete stop.

We could feel the ship's forward momentum slowing. The Explorer was still growing in our view screen but not nearly as fast as before.

"Reverse thrusters now," SC said.

I pressed the reverse thrust button. The reverse thrusters fired. I slowly eased up the button. The shuttle came to a complete stop. The Explorer was looming dead ahead of us.

GiS smiled at me though he tried not to show it.

"We are 900 kilometers away," Elvin said.

"Confirmed," SC said. "We are now within range for me to broadcast access codes to the Explorer."

"Begin broadcast," GiS said.

"Confirmed," SC said.

We all looked at the Explorer. At first nothing happened. Then a couple of the lights above the landing area blinked on. They weren't much, but they were a start.

"Is that it?" GiS asked.

"Wait for it," SC said.

One by one, more lights on the Explorer blinked to life, starting from the bottom and working their way up. Not all the lights came on, but at least half of them did. It still didn't look all that inviting but at least it didn't look dead anymore.

"How's that?" SC said.

"Is that all you can do?" GiS asked.

"Yes."

"In that case it will do," GiS said.

"I've also got life support going," SC said.

"That's good," I said. "Now can you open the landing bay door?"

"Of course," SC said. There was a pause. "Slight problem."

"Can you elaborate?" I asked.

"Yes," SC said.

We waited.

"Well?" GiS asked.

"I've got good news and bad news," SC said.

"What's the good news?" Zenna asked.

"I have gravity up in the Explorer and working at 75 percent, I have some lights working and life support working on minimal."

"If that's the good news, what's the bad?" I asked.

"Well," SC said slowly. "I can only get the bay door open 25 percent. Plus I can't activate any of the landing bay bots. For that matter I can't activate any of the bots aboard."

There was more silence.

"So we'll do it the old-fashioned way, without bots," Zenna said. "I'm sure back before bots, people landed on light-speed ships without bots."

Okay, her words didn't exactly make total sense, yet somehow they made enough sense. We were able to do this without bots. Sure, bots helped stop us. Sure, bots turned us around. Sure, bots loaded us with fuel. All of those were useful functions but we could get by without them.

"The shuttle can still fit in the door?" I asked.

"With over two meters to spare on each side," SC said.

"Let's do it," I said.

I looked over at GiS. He nodded and pointed forward. I started up the engines and eased her forward. It was funny. I was in a hurry to reach the Explorer, yet I wasn't in a hurry. I wanted to get it over with, to prove that I could do it. But I was also a little worried that I was in over my head. Landing on a mostly dead Explorer with the door mostly closed! Was I nuts?

I took a deep breath as we drew nearer and nearer to the Explorer. No, I wasn't crazy, nuts or loono. I was a galactic scout. I had a job to do and I was going to do it.

"This is going to be tricky," GiS said, not being all that helpful. "But quite doable," he added, trying to be helpful.

Normal procedure is to cut power 200 kilometers from your landing target and to drift in. Despite the fact that I was actually going quite slowly (by outer space speeds), I cut the power at 300 kilometers. I wanted to be extra careful. We didn't have to get there fast. We just needed to get there in one piece.

"You do realize there will be no computer assist on this landing," Elvin said.

"Yeah I know," I said as we closed the gap between us and the Explorer. "Computers are way overrated."

"Hey!" SC said.

"Nothing personal, SC," I said as we closed in on the Explorer.

Phew. There wasn't a lot of space. I was coming in a bit high. Normally there's no problem coming in a little high but this time there was no room for error. I lowered my ship's nose, then leveled her out. I held my breath (as I'm sure my crew as doing too).

The shuttle's nose entered the Explorer. So far so good. The body of the shuttle cleared the door; there were no explosions and no sparks. That was a good sign. We were in the landing bay. Since gravity was at 75 percent, the landing brakes should work just fine. I hoped.

I pressed the brake button. The shuttle slowed, but not as much as I thought it should have. We slid over my landing mark toward the far wall. The shuttle was slowly slowing down. The shuttle was going to stop. The question was, was it going to stop before it hit the wall?

We skidded across the floor.

"SC, are we going to stop?" I asked.

"Before we hit the wall?" SC asked, not being helpful.

"Preferably..." GiS said.

"The odds are good," SC said, slowly. "Three to one for."

"I agree, " Elvin said.

Those odds weren't good enough for me. The landing bay was empty so I had room to maneuver, so I figured I might as well use it. I pulled the control stick hard to the left, reversing the shuttle's direction. The shuttle jerked as it went to the left, but the movement not only gave us more room to move but it also slowed us down.

The shuttle rolled for a few hundred meters then came to a stop. Not the best landing. But it worked.

I looked at my crew. "Are you alright?"

Elvin and Zenna nodded.

"We're fine," GiS said. "Though the landing could have been smoother!"

"I thought you did a really good job, Baxter," Zenna said.

We all unharnessed and stood up. I stretched a bit. GiS

walked over to one of the shuttle's side panels. He pressed a few buttons with his feet. The side panel popped open. He pulled out five long rods — stun rods.

"Since we don't know what we're getting into I want us to at least be able to defend ourselves," GiS said.

He walked up to Zenna and handed her a stun energy rod.

"Thanks," she said.

He walked up to Elvin and handed him a rod. Elvin hesitated.

"I thought we weren't supposed to have weapons?"

"We can't have *lethal* weapons. These energy rods are locked on stun so they are only lethal to machines," GiS said.

Elvin smiled weakly. He opened his hand. GiS gave him a stun rod.

GiS tossed me a rod. I must have looked too eager as I caught it.

"Remember these are for emergency use only," GiS cautioned.

"Don't worry about me," I said as I walked toward the shuttle's door.

"It's..." GiS started to say.

"...my job to worry," Zenna, Elvin and I, said for him.

I reached for the door open button. I stopped. I looked up at SC.

"Are you sure life support is functioning?" I asked.

"Of course," SC said calmly. "Not at full capacity but at enough capacity so you'll be fine as long as you don't exert yourselves too much."

"That's reassuring," I said. I started to open the door again. I stopped again.

"What is it now?" SC asked.

"How are we going to communicate with you while we're on the ship?"

"I've patched SC into our intersquad sleeve communicators," Elvin said. "We can talk to him and he can talk to us."

"Are you happy now?" SC asked.

"Yep," I said.

I popped open the door.

Chapter 15

WE ALL DROPPED OUT OF THE SHUTTLE down the Explorer's landing bay. It had an eerie quiet about it. No bots running around. Just enough light to cast some freaky shadows and to let us see where we were going — barely.

We all kept our stun rods drawn as we slowly walked toward the elevator door. Our footsteps echoed off the vast emptiness of the room.

Elvin looked at a mini-scanner-computer he wore on his wrist. "Okay, the med lab is on the seventeenth floor," Elvin said.

We reached the elevator door. It didn't open.

"SC, can you activate the elevator?" GiS asked.

"Yes," SC said through our communicators.

We all waited. The door still didn't open.

"SC, will you activate the elevator?" GiS asked, exasperated.

"You don't want that," SC said.

"Why not?"

"Because in order to activate the elevator lift I would have to deactivate life support and gravity," SC said.

"Why didn't you tell us that before?"

"You didn't ask."

We all shook our heads in confusion. Well, all of us except Zenna. SC was acting a bit stranger than usual. My guess was that SC wasn't really designed to be powering a Space Sphere. Controlling two of them had put extra demand on his logic processors, making him a bit more flaky. At least I hoped that was the reason.

"I suggest you do this the old-fashioned way," SC said. "There is a man-powered-vertical-rung-lift that runs along the left side the elevator."

Sure enough, on closer examination the wall on to the left of the lift did appear to have a removable panel. Elvin tapped the panel with his rod. It gave off a hollow sound.

Elvin ran his hand up and down the wall.

"I can't seem to find a switch to give us access," he said.

Zenna stepped up to the wall.

"Here — it needs a lady's touch," she said.

Zenna grabbed hold of the panel. There were no grip bars or slots but Zenna made two by literally digging her hands into the wall. She groaned for a second, then pulled back, pulling the panel off the wall. She turned and tossed the panel into the bay area. She rubbed her hands together cleaning off the dust. She smiled.

"A woman's work is never done," she said happily.

Behind the panel was a small room not much bigger than a closet. There was also a ladder leading straight up, way up.

We all walked into the room. We looked up. All we could see was ladder.

"Each level has exactly 125 rungs," SC said briskly. "When you reach a level there is a door that is clearly marked that leads to the floor. I suggest you start now."

GiS looked up at the ladder and smiled. "I haven't had a workout like this in a while!" he said enthusiastically. "This will be good for us."

"It will be like climbing to the top of the old Empire State building," Elvin said.

GiS pointed to the ladder. "Zenna, you lead the way because we might need your muscle to open the door."

"Right," Zenna said. She grabbed the ladder and started moving up.

"Baxter and Elvin, you two are next. I'll follow up the rear. Just in case I have to give one of you a little push."

I grabbed the ladder and looked up. All I could see was more ladder. I decided it was best not to look. I started up.

"Remember, don't look down," GiS shouted.

———————

After about an hour's worth of climbing, we had reached the tenth floor. Zenna was a trooper as always. She didn't show any signs of tiring. Her only concern was that she had to be careful not to fart with all of us behind her like we were.

GiS of course was eating this up. He loved it. Of course it's easy to climb when you can grab the rungs with either your feet or your hands.

I had to give Elvin credit. He hated heights. Yet he was hanging in there. He was sweating like a pig but he was keeping up with us without much prodding from GiS. He was also working out ways that SC would be able to activate the elevator for the ride down without having to deactivate gravity or life support.

As for me, I was much more worried about the boredom killing me than anything else. The climb was strenuous, but nothing I couldn't handle. Like some dead philosopher once said, whatever doesn't kill us makes us stronger. Part of me, though, was craving action. The other part of me, the smaller, more cautious, part had a feeling that soon there would be plenty of action.

We climbed and climbed. Each level had a little walk pad and door marked with the floor number on it. We would take a brief two-minute break on every fifth pad. After about another hour (that felt a lot longer) we reached the walk pad for the seventeenth floor.

We all stood on the pad. Elvin looked at his scanner.

"The energy reading is down this hall," he said.

"Any extra energy readings?" GiS asked.

Elvin shook his head no.

Zenna pushed the door open. We all peered down the hallway. It didn't look like much, a long dark hall, dotted by doors.

"The med lab is at the very end of the hall," Elvin said.

"Of course it is," I said. "Anyplace else wouldn't be as creepy."

We started walking down the hallway. Zenna, GiS and I had our weapons ready. Elvin was working out some calculations on his scanner.

"Are you still picking up energy readings, Elvin?" GiS asked as we moved closer to the door in question.

"Huh?" Elvin said as GiS's words pulled him away from his wrist scanner. He pressed another button. "Uh, yes," Elvin said.

We continued down the hallway until we came to the door. GiS looked at the access pad on the door.

"SC, do you know what the door's access code is?"

"Yes."

"What is it?" GiS asked anxiously.

"It doesn't matter."

"Why not?"

"The door is not locked."

"Why didn't you say so in the first place?"

"You never asked."

GiS just shook his head and mumbled, "Computers..."

I'm pretty sure SC mumbled back, "Chimps..." But we all ignored it.

GiS pressed the open button. The door sprang open. Sure enough, the room was a med room. In the middle of the room was a stasis bed. We were all familiar enough with stasis beds; every ship had them. They would put you in a state of almost suspended animation. In the old days these beds, which looked pretty much like a standard regulation bed enclosed in a big tube, were used to help pass the time during long space flights. These days, the beds are used for healing. It has been found that the body heals much more rapidly while in near suspended state.

So the stasis bed wasn't anything special. What was special was what was in the bed. Or should I say, who was in the bed. It was a blue-skinned, blue-haired girl, wearing a long dark green dress with sequins on it. She looked like she was about our age.

We all approached the bed cautiously. None of us had ever seen an alien before. At least not this close.

"Zow! An Aquarian!" Zenna said.

"Dah, do you think?" Elvin said cynically.

"Yes, I do," Zenna said, sincerely. "Gee, Elvin you're pretty smart, you should have been able to figure that out!" Zenna studied the girl's fine features a bit. "Wow, she's really beautiful," she said.

"Hush!" GiS ordered.

"Why — are you afraid we might wake her?" I asked.

GiS shook his head. "No, it's just proper protocol to do these things quietly!"

"Oh," Zenna said softly.

GiS looked at the control pad at the side of the bed. "We've got to get her out of here, stat."

None of us was going to argue.

"SC, what's the code to resuscitate her and open the bed?" GiS asked.

"The code letters are W-A-K-E-U-P," SC said.

"You're kidding," I said.

"I never kid when it comes to access codes," SC said.

GiS punched in the code. We all waited a tic. A white mist entered the tube enclosing the bed. The mist cleared. The tube opened up. The girl started to cough. She opened her eyes.

"Humans!"

Elvin leaned over the bed. "We're here to save you!" Elvin said in his most macho voice. It wasn't all that macho.

"Well, you're not doing a very good job of it!" the girl said. She sat up and lunged forward to grab Elvin's stun rod. Before any of us could do anything she fired the rod. The laser blast flew past us all and into a little medical bot. Unbeknownst to any of us, the bot had snuck up on us and was getting ready to inject us with one of its syringe arms.

The blast from the rod short-circuited the bot. It vibrated violently, then fell over.

"Nice shot!" I said.

"The entire Aquarian royal family are excellent shots," she said proudly. "I'm actually glad you were smart enough to bring weapons. Though they do break our agreement." She stretched.

We all looked at the princess. She was cocky, but Zenna was correct she was attractive, especially if you liked blue skin, long hair, long eye lashes and perfectly formed lips — which I did. She certainly didn't seem very grateful, considering we had just saved her butt. I guess she saved ours too, though, from the medbot's syringe.

"You shouldn't have come," she said. "The creatures you call the TVTrons are in control of the bots on this ship. They attacked my ship and this ship with some sort of reprogramming ray! It turned our computers and our bots against us. Once we were helpless, the TVTrons boarded our ships and took us away."

I had to give the princess points for being spunky. She had the air of a person who never thought she was wrong. She kind of reminded me of Kymm.

"Why are you on the Explorer?" GiS asked. The rest of us (well, except for probably Zenna) were thinking the same thing.

She shook her head. "The TVTrons' mind control ray did not work on me. So they left me here in suspended animation."

"Why didn't they just kill you?" Elvin asked.

"My guess is they wanted to see what makes my brain different from everybody else's before they start their full-scale attacks. I also guess they figured I'd be easier to hold here in stasis than up on their mother pyramid ship."

"They didn't count on us figuring out how to stop their reprogramming ray and coming to rescue you!" Elvin said.

The Aquarian girl hopped off the bed and stretched again. She was tall and in good shape, really good shape if you get what I am talking about. "Some rescue," she said coldly. "You're in the middle of ship surrounded by hostile machines."

"She's right," GiS said. "We have to get off of this ship sooner than ASAP."

"That will be much easier said than accomplished," SC said. "Currently the hallway between her and the exit is filled with bots. And they aren't here to serve you." SC paused for a tic. "Except maybe to the TVTrons."

"Like I said before, nice rescue, humans," the girl said mockingly.

"Actually, before you said, *some rescue*," Zenna said as only Zenna could.

The Aquarian girl looked at Zenna. "My, you're one of the smarter Earthers," she said.

"Thanks!" Zenna said.

The Aquarian girl just shook her head.

"What's your name?" Elvin asked.

"I am Princess Amana of the royal government. You may address me as Your Highness," she said grandly.

Before anybody could respond, a cylinder-shaped maidbot rolled into the room. "Surrender, humans!" it shouted as loudly as a maidbot could. "Or I will be forced to hurt you."

"Please, what are you going to do? Dust us to death?" Elvin said.

Sure enough two dusters popped out of the bot's sides. They didn't look all that intimidating. The bot started to whirl the duster heads like buzz saws. Suddenly they looked pretty intimidating.

The bot whirled toward us.

I aimed. I fired. My shot hit the bot. The bot stumbled backwards, crackling with electricity! "I'm hit! I'm hit!!" it shouted. It spun around in circles and then went dead.

"That was just plain weird," Zenna said.

"My theory is the bots aren't used to being controlled by the TVTrons, plus these bots weren't built to be fighting bots so they really don't know how to act," Elvin said.

"Yes, but they managed to overwhelm my people and your people," the princess said.

"Yes, but we're armed," GiS said.

"Yes, but you are outnumbered 100 to 1," SC said bluntly. "You still stand little chance."

The princess just shook her head. "You are going to end up with the TVTrons just like the others."

GiS gave her a polite bow. "Don't worry, Princess, uh, Your Highness, we're going to get you out of here and back to the Searcher. Then we'll head back to Earth so you can tell both worlds what happened."

The princess stamped her foot on the floor. "No!" she shouted. "I am a high princess in the Aquarian government. Even if by some miracle upon miracles you do get off this ship, I can't leave my people captured on the TVTrons' mother ship." She crossed her arms defiantly.

I looked at the princess. She wasn't going to budge. I looked at GiS; if he wasn't fur covered he would have been blood red. He wasn't use to being talked to like this. He was one tic from pardon the pun, going ape. I had to step in to prevent an inter-planetary incident. Besides, I've never been one to let a pretty girl down, even if she was a bossy alien with blue hair.

"Listen, princess..." I said in my most diplomatic voice.

"Your Highness, please," the princess interrupted.

"We can't rescue your people if we can't get off the ship, uh, Your Highness. Correct?"

The princess folded her arms even tighter. "Yes, that is quite obvious, Earther." "Then this is my promise to you," I said.

"We all get off this robot-controlled ship and back to our ship. From there we'll make plans to rescue your people and our people."

The princess became a little less rigid. "I suppose that plan does make some sense," she said. "What is your name?" she asked, though it was more of a demand than a question.

"Baxter Moon, Galactic Scout Second Class," I said.

She smiled. It was the first time I had seen any crack in her stony façade. "Well, Baxter Moon, Galactic Scout Second Class, you show surprising composure for a commoner."

"Thanks, I think."

"Now tell me, Baxter Moon, what is our next step?"

GiS, who had been quietly watching this unfolding, couldn't bear it any longer. "I'm in command here," he said.

The princess glared at him. "No, Animal, I am in command here! I am a member of the Aquarian royal family and world council. We do not recognize your authority."

I vaguely remember them teaching us in alien culture awareness class that Aquarians were against Earth's practice of modifying animals to make them more like us. They considered the practice to be unnatural (which it was) and barbaric. Of course our professor said that was all just hearsay. But the princess's actions made hearsay reality. She was showing true contempt for GiS, like he was even further beneath her than we were.

I had to do something fast. We couldn't have much more time before the bots came crashing into this room. Then we'd be dead ducks — trapped, sitting dead ducks.

"Princess, I know your people don't agree with what some of my people do with animals," I said.

"It's unnatural, Baxter Moon. And 'Your Highness,' please. This chimp should be running free in the wild, not dressed up as a space chimp."

"Uh, there isn't that much wild left on Earth," Elvin said, not really helping.

"Then he should be in a habitat! He should not be in command of humans!"

GiS was now really taken aback. He was getting ready to let the animal inside of him out. I knew, though, that no good could come from him going ape on the princess. Maybe the princess had a point. Maybe animals shouldn't be in charge. After all no matter how much we "improve" them, who's to say if our improvements are really improvements? Can we really take the animal out of the animal? Even if we could, do we want to?

However, this wasn't the time and certainly not the situation for me to suddenly start thinking about the big questions. I had to focus on the task at hand — getting these two to cooperate so we could get out of here.

I locked eyes with the princess. Wow, she had nice eyes! They didn't look through you quite as much as Commander Jasmine's, still they were soft yet powerful, nearly hypnotic.

I shook my head. I had to keep my eyes off the princess and on the goal. "Princess, I understand your feelings. Believe me, I really understand them. But GiS is very intelligent and I value his opinion."

I turned to GiS. "If you really are as intelligent as I think you are, you will be able to see the princess's point of view."

They stood there glaring at each other. You didn't have to be an expert in animal to alien relationships to see neither of them would be starting a fan club for the other.

"Look, you two don't have to get married, or even like each other, just get along," I coaxed.

The princess looked at me. "Fine, I can not help my people if I die here." She held out her hand palm down. She was expecting GiS to kiss it, though it was easy to see she wasn't thrilled by the possibility.

GiS looked at the outstretched hand. He wasn't thrilled with the possibility of his lips touching her hand.

"Baxter Moon, the voice of reason," GiS said slowly. "Who would have thunk it."

He touched the princess's hand ever so slightly with his. They both seemed to prefer this to the hand kiss. They gave each other weak smiles.

"Great! Now can we get out of here, before these bots break in and break us?" Zenna asked.

Zenna had picked up the slack. She had bolted the door shut and was leaning against it making sure that no bots would have easy access to us.

The door was heavy metal so we couldn't see how many bots were now in the hallway but we could hear them. They were banging on the door, clamoring to get in.

The princess looked at the door, she looked at me. "So, Baxter Moon, Galactic Scout," she said. "What is your plan for getting us out of here alive?"

Now, that was a good question. I always pride myself of being able to think fast on my feet. It was time to prove to myself that my pride was justified. The bots had managed to over-power the crew of the Explorer, but we had a couple of things going for us that they didn't. For one thing, we were armed. For another, and probably more important, our computer was still functioning.

"Zen, how many bots do you think are out there?" I asked.

Zenna leaned her ear against the door to listen. "I don't know..." she said meekly.

"Guess," I said.

Zenna shrugged. "Lots?"

"Can you be more specific?"

"I can be more specific but not more accurate," Zenna said.

"Let's just hope none of them have access to laser drills," Elvin said.

"SC, how many bots are in the hallway?" I asked.

"Lots," SC said.

I shook my head. "You have to be more specific than that!"

"I only have access to one section of the hallway's internal cameras. I can extrapolate the number of bots in the hall based on that sample and the size of the hallway but it would not be as accurate as I would like."

"Rough guess," I said.

"I am a computer, I do not guess."

"Rough extrapolation then." I said.

"One hundred and three."

I took a deep breath. I reviewed our advantages: we were armed and had a working computer. Plus we had Zenna's muscles, Elvin's brains, GiS's coordination.

"Come on, Baxter," the princess said, touching me on the shoulder. "We need to get out of here! I do not wish to have my people at the mercy of the TVTrons for one time unit more."

I guess we also had the princess's spunk on our side, but I wasn't really sure how much help that would be.

"SC, can you send conflicting orders to the bots?"

"I do have some access to their control network. But what do you mean by conflicting orders?"

"Tell them to move left and move right at the same time," I said.

"I can mimic their master computer, but it will only fool them for a short time."

"That will have to be enough," I said. "When they are confused, we rush out the door, blast them to the side and run for our shuttle."

"That's your plan?" the princess shouted. "To run?" She pointed at GiS. "Maybe we should hear what the animal has to offer?"

"Well..." GiS said.

"I wasn't serious," the princess said.

I was starting to kind of like this princess.

Elvin spoke up. "We'll never make it down the ladder. We'll be way too vulnerable."

"What other option do we have?" I asked.

"I'm glad you asked," Elvin said with a smile. "Now that I've had a chance to run some numbers, I've figured we can power the lift. We just don't need life support."

We all looked at him.

Elvin went on, his face covered by a huge smile. "We cut life support and use the saved energy to power the lift. It's a quick trip down. So we just hold our breath. Then when we hit the bay, we reactivate life support, fight our way to the shuttle and get out of here."

It certainly wasn't the best plan I ever heard. But it was going to have to do. We could hear the bots grinding and pounding against the door. We had to act now.

I looked at the door. I looked at Zenna leaning on the door.

"Zenna, give your stun rod to the princess."

"Okay."

Zenna tossed her rod to the princess though I could see from her face she wasn't entirely at ease about it.

I walked over to Zenna and put my hand on her shoulder. "You don't need the rod because we're going to be using the Zenna-dozer to get out of here."

Zenna looked at me even more confused than usual.

"Dozer isn't my last name," she said.

"We're going to use you as a bulldozer and the door as shield."

Zenna gave me her deer in the headlights look.

"You're going to kick the door down. That should take out the bots by the door. Then you pick up the door and use it as a shield and plow as we push the bots down the hall away from the lift. The rest of us will be behind you, picking off any bots that get behind us or can't be plowed away."

My team and the princess just looked at me. They weren't exactly brimming with confidence.

"It will work," I said.

"If Baxter Moon says it will work, then I believe him," the princess said.

Zenna nodded her head. "That's right, Baxter has been our leader and we're all still alive."

"He did kill us a couple of times in simulation," Elvin pointed out.

Zenna looked dazed and then said, "Well this is life, not a simulation. If we die here, we really die. So it's different and Baxter knows that." Zenna looked at me. "Right, Baxter?"

I didn't really know what to say. Elvin was right. I had screwed up in simulations. Zenna was also right in her own Zenna way. This wasn't a simulation or a drill. I knew that. I would be taking no undue chances with the lives of my crew and the beautiful princess. Besides, I didn't see a lot of options here. Then why did I feel so uneasy here?

Finally GiS spoke up. "Baxter is right. It's our only way out of here!"

I don't know why but hearing GiS say that was the extra confidence boost I needed.

"Okay, everybody but Zenna, energy rods ready!" I ordered.

They all powered up their rods and pointed them at the door.

"Okay, SC," I said. "Do what you can to confuse the bots!"

"I am emitting contradicting orders," SC said. "I am telling them to go right and left at the same time."

I pointed my hand at the door.

"Zenna, bring the door down!" I ordered.

"Hit the top of the door, right then left," Elvin said. "That should cause it to land on top of any bots in front of it without letting them get through."

"Gotcha. I mean check," Zenna said.

Zenna made a fist with her left hand. She pounded her fist into the upper right corner of the door, jarring the door loose. She quickly pounded her fist into the upper left corner of the door, the door crashed to the floor, flattening a bunch of bots underneath.

Between SC sending conflicting orders and Zenna sending the door down on them, the bots were now doubly confused. Zenna took advantage of their confusion, leaping into the hallway. She picked up the door and flicked it with her wrists. The force of the flick cleared out any of the nearby bots that had survived the initial crush from the door. Zenna held the door upright, using it to cut off any more bots.

She turned to all of us in the doorway. "Let's go," she said.

We followed Zenna into the hall and down the hall as she slowly pushed her way forward. We all had our weapons pointed, charged and ready, but we didn't need them. Since the med lab was at the end of the hall there were no bots behind us to begin with. With Zenna pushing the door the bots had no way to get by her because the door was just wide enough to block the hallway. Even if the bots weren't confused, there wasn't much they could do to stop or even slow down Zenna.

We plodded forward, Zenna pushing and the rest of us watching her back. It was an impressive sight. We actually weren't going that much slower than we would have been if we had been walking unimpeded.

The princess was impressed. "Are all human females this powerful?" she asked.

"This is nothing," Elvin said. "You want power, wait until she takes her boots off!"

My confidence was growing with each passing step as we pushed closer and closer to the lift. This was turning out to be easier than I expected.

We heard rustling from the floor above us. The rustling stopped and was replaced by the sound of sawing. I should have known better than to think this was going to be a cakewalk. I actually had no idea what a cakewalk was but I knew this wasn't going to be one.

GiS pointed up toward the sawing sound. "Drill bots," he said. "They are going to use the ducts to drop in behind us."

Sure enough, almost on GiS's words the ceiling tile above and behind us fell to the floor. A big drill bot dropped behind us. This was the type of bot used for deep space mining, basically two huge drills on the top of tank tracks guided with sensors. These drills were meant to bore through solid rock crusts of barren planets. They were now spinning toward us. Each drill head was bigger than each of our heads.

Elvin and GiS were both guarding the rear so they were the two closest to the approaching drill bots. Elvin was trembling as he aimed his energy rod. In fact he was so scared by the approaching bot, his first shot sailed over its head. GiS's shot was much truer. It hit the bot directly in the drill. Unlike the other bots though, this bot kept coming.

Elvin gulped. "These bots are built to operate on planets with heavy electrical storm activity," he said as only a geek could. "Our energy rods won't stop them."

"Not if we use them like energy rods," GiS said.

He grabbed Elvin's energy rod as he leapt forward at the attacking bot. The bot bore its drills down at GiS. GiS jumped over the drills to behind the bot just as the drill heads bore down on the floor. Sometimes it pays to be a chimp.

GiS pointed his energy rod at the bot, but instead of firing at it, he jammed the rod into the bot's tread. Drill bots may have been built for tough terrain but they weren't meant to stand up to an attack from an intelligent chimp. The bot lurched forward, now totally off balance thanks to the energy rod jammed in its treads. The bot tipped forward embedding its drills into the floor and wedging itself stuck. GiS smiled and hopped back over the bot.

Two other drill bots dropped down but it would take them a while to get past the wedged-in bot.

"Come on! Let's move!" GiS shouted.

We pushed forward until we reached the lift door.

"Okay, SC, open the lift," I shouted.

"You don't have to shout," SC said. "I can hear you just fine over your communicator."

The door popped open.

The princess went in first, followed by Elvin and GiS.

"Okay, Zenna, we don't need the shield anymore. Push the door down on the bots and jump in."

Zenna pushed the door forward. The door tipped over, crushing the nearest bots. She dove into the lift. A couple of the bots just behind the reach of the door managed to get off energy blasts at her. One of the blasts nicked her in the arm. I finished the bots off with two quick energy blasts of my own and then jumped into the lift.

I fired off a few more shots just as the door zoomed closed.

"I assume you want to go to the shuttle bay," SC said.

"That would be quite logical," I said.

I turned and looked at Zenna. Her uniform was torn at her shoulder and she was bleeding a bit. She was covered with sweat. She had never looked better to me.

"Are you okay?" I asked.

"I'm fine," she said. "It will take more than a bunch of buggy bots to stop me."

"That's our Zenna," I said.

"Okay, everybody hold their breath," GiS ordered.

We all inhaled.

"Life support off, lift on," SC said.

We felt the lift descending. The lift stopped its descent. We all looked at each other.

"We have reached the landing bay," SC said. "Life support is back."

We exhaled. The door popped up.

"Wait!" I yelled to SC. "Don't open the door until..."

"No need to yell or worry," SC reassured us. "The bay is bot free."

Sure enough, as we carefully peeked out over the bay, the place looked empty. Our shuttle was sitting there all alone, nice and peaceful. It was freaky.

We stepped out into the bay. Weapons drawn, ready for anything. But we found nothing.

We headed toward our shuttle.

"It's quiet," Elvin said. "Too quiet."

We all glared at him. Elvin smiled. "I always wanted to say that."

We moved closer to the shuttle. Zenna was in the lead, followed by the princess and me with GiS and Elvin bringing up the rear. We reached the shuttle. Elvin pointed his scanner at the shuttle.

"My readings don't detect any bot activity in there," Elvin said.

We walked up to the shuttle door. Despite Elvin's assurances, it still didn't feel right. We all just looked at the door's access code panel. It was a weird feeling. We certainly didn't want to stay here. But it just seemed too easy to be able to get on the shuttle and fly out of here.

Elvin shook his head. "I told you guys it's clean!" He walked up and entered the door's access code. The door slid open. Elvin ducked in.

"Greetings, Humans," a robot voice said.

"TVTrons!" the princess shouted.

Chapter 16

A BEAM OF LIGHT HIT ELVIN in the face before any of us could do anything. Elvin sat on the shuttle floor with a goofy smile on his face. "Entertain me," he said.

The rest of us rushed into the shuttle. There were two TVTrons in there, one in front of the other. They looked identical, big old-fashioned TV screens with a projector on top. The TV "head" sat on top of a little wheeled base with claw arms sticking out of it. They looked far more ridiculous than threatening. We aimed our energy rods at the TVTrons. A smile appeared across the lead TVTron's screen.

"Good humans," it said, in a high-pitched voice. "Now, you WILL be entertained!"

"Not quite," I said. I pointed my energy rod at the TVTron and pressed the fire button.

"Your shuttle deactivated all your weapons," the TVTron said cheerfully.

It was right. I had forgotten that. Zam! A good leader doesn't forget details like that, even if they only heard it once in a class a couple of years ago.

Elvin just sat there staring at the static on the screen of the lead TVTron.

"You will now all be entertained," the other TVTron said.

"You forgot, I am immune to your ray!" the princess said.

"You forgot we captured you once; we will capture you again, " the TVTron said.

Zenna moved forward and raised her fist.

"Nobody takes over my brother's brain!" she shouted.

The lead TVTron aimed its projector at Zenna. The beam hit her in the eyes. Zenna smiled. She opened her fist. She sat down, legs crossed and started staring at the screen.

"See," one of the TVTrons said, "resistance is futile."

There are times when you have to think before you react. There are times when you have to react without thinking. This was one of those times. I raised my energy rod over my head and then threw it like a make-shift spear at the lead TVTron. The rod pieced right through its screen. It shattered; the TVTron went limp.

My mom always told me that throwing the javelin on the track team would pay off for me someday. Who would have ever thought she was right?

"That's not how this plot is suppose to go!" the remaining TVTron shouted. "The producer will not be pleased!"

Before the TVTron could do anything, I grabbed GiS's energy rod and flung it through its screen. The TVTron stopped shouting. It curled over and fell to the floor.

Elvin and Zenna both shook their heads and came out of their trance.

"What the...?" Elvin said.

"It was like a dream, a weird dream," Zenna said. "And I have some weird dreams."

I tapped them on the shoulders. "Come on guys, stand up," I said. "We've got to get out of here, pronto."

Elvin looked at the shattered TVTrons. "What happened?" he said.

"I canceled their show," I said.

Elvin scanned the deleted TVTrons with his sleeve communicator (which also functions as a scanner, calculator and music player). "No signs of life," he said.

"Should I throw them out?" Zenna asked, standing up.

"No, their frames might be useful to us," GiS said.

"What?" the princess said. "How can you want to keep them?"

"GiS's right," I said. "We can learn a lot from these." I moved past the dead trons and took the pilot's seat.

The princess smiled. "If you say so, Baxter, then I will go along," she said.

"Come on, let's get out of here!" I said.

My crew took their seats and the princess sat in one of the shuttle's extra seats. I could tell she wasn't happy being in the back of the shuttle, but she was smart enough not to complain about it, at least for now. I fired up the engine. I was anxious to get out of the Explorer to the quiet peace of space. I maneuvered the shuttle around so it was facing the bay door we came in through.

"Okay, SC, open the bay door," I commanded.

"As you may recall I can not completely open the door," SC said.

"Just do what you can as quickly as you can," I said.

The door slowly drew open. Well, not totally open, of course but half open.

I eased the shuttle forward toward the door. Before we got halfway to the door, it started to close. I should have expected it, but I was still surprised.

"SC, we're not out yet! Don't close the door," I said.

"I am not in control of the door," SC said.

I looked at the door. It was closing much more rapidly than it had opened. I hit the throttle. The ship rocketed forward.

"You're going too fast!" GiS shouted.

"I don't see any other options," I answered calmly, keeping my ship steady.

We shot through the door, a brief tic or two before it slammed shut. I looked at my aft view screen. As the Explorer grew smaller on the screen, I was growing more confident. We had done it! We had found a way to stop the war. We could take the princess back to Earth and let her explain to everybody what had happened. We could then let Earth Force take care of the TVTrons.

"I can now establish communication with the Searcher," SC said.

"Put her through," GiS said.

"Shuttle Sigma, this is the Searcher. Nice to see you made it out," K-999 said,

"Nice to be out," GiS answered.

"SC tells us you've picked up a friend," K-999 said.

"We'll be on board in less than five minutes and you can all meet her," I said.

For once in my life I was happy with the way things turned out. Of course I knew my happiness couldn't last long.

Chapter 17

WHEN WE LANDED ON THE SEARCHER, we were greeted by the entire Kappa team. As soon as I got out of the shuttle, K-999 gave me a paw pat on the back.

"Nice job, boy. I always knew you had it in you," he said.

K-999 looked carefully at Princess Amana. He bowed his head. "Princess."

I could see the princess wasn't any more comfortable with K-999 as she was with GiS. Still he was being polite to her so she decided to at least acknowledge him.

"Dog," she said, trying at least a little to hold back the contempt in her voice. "You may address me as Your Highness...if you have to."

Lobi and Chriz just ogled the princess while Kymm gave her the once- or twice-over. The princess walked up to Lobi and Chriz. They both put their hands behind their backs and stood there like lovesick schoolboys (which I guess they were.)

The princess looked at Kymm. "Do these two talk?"

"Usually I can't get them to shut up," Kymm said.

The princess looked at them. "For some reason I like it this way. You should keep them like this."

"Now that you are back and with the princess we can get back to Earth and stop this war!" K-999 said.

The princess stopped in her tracks. "No!" she shouted. "I will not go to Earth…"

"Why not? Earth is a nice planet!" Zenna said.

"I'm sure they will return you to Aqua," Kymm said, being more helpful.

"I will not go to Aqua either," the princess said, pounding her foot into the floor. "Not when my people are prisoners of those TVTrons!"

"But princess, if we don't get back soon there could be war," GiS said.

The princess shook her head. "We have time," she insisted. She looked at me, with those big brown eyes and batted her lashes. "Don't we, Baxter? After all, your people are missing too."

I thought about what she said (trying not to take her looks into account). She was right; we did have people lost and chances are they were somewhere in this sector of space. Still, we could send the army here. It was more up their line.

The princess smiled at me. That was it.

"I think we can hang around a day or two longer," I said. "Maybe we can find our people."

"How do you propose we do that?" K-999 asked.

Okay, I didn't have an answer for that one. Lucky for me, Lobi did.

"I think I found them," Lobi said meekly.

"What," Chriz said. "How?"

"With the information SC was able to give us about Explorer's systems I was able to find them."

"Really?" GiS asked.

Lobi nodded. "I need another hour or two before I'm sure." He pointed at Elvin, "plus I could use Elvin's help."

"You've got it," GiS said. "We will meet in conference room 1A in three hours. Until then, Baxter, Zenna, the princess and I can freshen up."

"What about me?" Elvin asked. "When can I freshen up?"

"After the mission," GiS said.

"Man, the price I pay for being a brain," Elvin sulked.

One of the bots rolled up to the princess. Before the bot could do anything, she grabbed my energy rod and shot it. The bot burst into flames.

"Ah, princess, uh, Your Highness," I said, cautiously. "Here on this ship we still have control of the bots."

"Oh," she said, looking at the wrecked bot. "Sorry about that."

"What the bot was going to say is, we've assigned her the room across from Baxter's," SC said.

The princess smiled. "That will be fine."

She offered me her arm. "Now you may escort me to my quarters."

I took her arm. I liked it. Walking away I felt Kymm's eyes on me too. I liked that also. Man, who would have thought fighting evil TVTrons would have been so good for my potential love life? For now though, I had to concentrate on saving two worlds. I escorted the princess up the lift and to her room.

I entered the access code into her door and the door popped open. I showed her the room much like a game show host would show a contestant a prize they had won.

"Not exactly the royal suite," I said.

She smiled. "As you Earth people say, desperate times call for desperate actions," she said.

We both entered the room. "Now remember, Your Highness, the bots on this ship are under our control so you don't have to destroy them all."

The princess sat down on the bed. She bounced on it softly, checking how firm it was. "Ha ha," she said, "you are very funny, like your planet's Jerry Lewis."

I gave her a blank look. "Who?"

"Have you not heard of him? He is probably your planet's greatest gift to humor. He was very popular one hundred of your years ago."

"Sorry, I don't watch the ancient stuff."

She shook her head. "Too bad, you lose so much of your culture that way."

I couldn't be sure she was serious, but I was pretty certain she was.

The princess and I just sat there and talked as the time flew by. I knew I should have been sleeping or resting but I wasn't tired. In fact I felt exhilarated. I don't know if it was from freeing the princess or from hanging out with her. But whatever the reason, I felt better about myself than I had in a long time. If not better than I had ever felt.

The next thing I knew, it was time to head to the conference room.

———

I was surprised to see that the princess and I were the first ones in the conference room. As surprised as I was, though, I think GiS and K-999 were even more shocked when they walked in a few minutes after us.

GiS looked at me like he couldn't believe his eyes. K-999 even sniffed the air to make sure it was really us.

"Why are they looking at us like that?" the princess said.

"They're not used to me being early for a meeting," I said.

"Ah, so you are always late because you are busy planning your strategy," she said earnestly.

"Yeah that's it."

Kymm, Zenna and Chriz entered the room. Each of them had a look that was a cross between amazement and bewilderment on their faces.

"Oh man, we're late," Kymm said.

"No we're not," Chriz said pointing to the digital holographic clock on the wall. "Baxter was just early."

Zenna just smiled.

The three sat down. Zenna just kept smiling at me. Kymm was smiling too, only it was a less sincere smile. Chriz wasn't even pretending to smile. It was eating him up that I was getting all this attention.

Before I had a chance to rub the attention I was getting in Chriz's face, Lobi and Elvin came bursting into the room. Lobi was even more hyper than normal.

"I found them! I found them!" he shouted, almost hyperventilating.

"Slow down, Scout," K-999 growled.

"We used the information SC obtained while we were on Explorer." Lobi was now turning red in the face with excitement.

"They are cloaked but we can see them," Elvin said, only slightly less excited than Lobi.

"Where are they?" GiS asked.

"They were on the Explorer all along," Lobi said. "We picked up thirty-two organic life signs. They are all in the first floor conference room."

"Are you sure?" Kymm asked.

Elvin and Lobi both shrugged. "This is science. You can never be sure, but it's highly probable."

"Why didn't we notice those life signs before?" GiS asked.

"We didn't have sensors tuned to be so sensitive," Elvin said.

"Or this could be a way to lure us in. To trap us," GiS said.

"Of course it could be a trap, Animal," the princess snapped. "But we still have to go."

"She's right, you know," I said. "We've got to chance it."

"There's no way we can fit thirty-two beings on one shuttle," Kymm said.

"Then we'll take both shuttles," I said.

"We'll have no backup!" Chriz said.

"If we fail, then Searcher heads for Earth and sends Earth Force," Kymm said.

"We'll need at least two of us to stay on Searcher," K-999 said.

"I'll stay with Lobi," GiS said.

Lobi breathed a big sigh of relief. He was none too anxious to actually face the TVTrons, being much more of a "theory" than a "practice" type of guy than the rest of us. He actually made Elvin look like a jock. GiS, though, surprised me. I wasn't so surprised that he didn't mind missing the action. I was surprised that he trusted me enough to fly a shuttle on a dangerous mission without him.

GiS looked me in the eye. "I'm sure the princess will take my seat."

The princess swallowed. "It would be an honor," she said.

K-999 shook his head. "Sigma, are you sure you're up to making two trips in one day?"

"I'll rest when I'm dead," I said.

"I'll be fine," Elvin said. "Though I wish Baxter had picked his words a little differently."

"Ditto, ditto," Zenna said.

I smiled. That was my team. Sticking by me through thick and thin. Even if they weren't sure I was right, if I was sure I was right, they were willing to trust me. I wasn't about to make any of us wrong.

K-999 looked at GiS. "You sure you're sure?"

"I see no other options, my friend."

"Fine. We'll take off in one hour."

You know how when you're really anxious for something, time just seems to crawl? Well, the hour before take off seemed to last a lifetime. I know why I was anxious. I knew the TVTrons would be waiting for us. We had barely escaped the last time and now were going in again. I guess I just wanted to get it over with one way or another.

It was funny hanging out with the princess. She was sort of pompous and arrogant, not the type of girl I thought I'd find myself attracted to, but I did. I wasn't sure what that said about me. Maybe I saw the deeper, committed leader in her? Maybe it was because she was so pretty? Maybe I just liked the attention? But whatever the reason, I kind of liked the way I felt when I was around her. It was like I could take anything the universe could throw at me.

I liked hanging with her.

The princess looked at me as we walked into the shuttle bay. "You seem nervous, Baxter."

"Nah, just cautious."

She stared at me.

"Okay, maybe I'm a little nervous."

"No need to be nervous. You are a great pilot and fast thinker on your feet. We will be fine."

"Gee, princess, uh, Your Highness, now you sound like Zenna."

The princess stopped walking. She cocked her head back. "I'm not sure how I should take that..."

"It's meant to be a compliment," I said, motioning for her to come along.

We walked up to my shuttle, where the bots were just finishing prepping her for flight. My crew was already in the shuttle.

Kymm was walking around her shuttle, just finishing her preflight check. Kymm didn't trust her crew or the bots as much as I did. Which is fine, we all have our own styles. Plus, with Kymm's special eye, she could detect small cuts and dinks that others couldn't. Kymm turned to the princess and me and gave me a thumbs up and wink, then went into her shuttle.

"That girl likes you," the princess said with a sly smile.

"We're both pilots," I said, as I started walking around my shuttle, looking for anything that might not be quite right. (I trust my crew and the bots, but it's not a blind trust.) "We're friends, nothing more."

The princess just smiled.

I finished my inspection and joined my crew in the shuttle.

Zenna was at her station checking her instruments. Elvin was at his station but he wasn't checking his consoles. He was using a mini-laser on a strange-looking pair of sun glasses.

"Ah, Elvin we're in space, millions of miles away from any sun. You don't need shades," I told him.

He looked up from his work. He gave me his I'm-a-genius-I-know-that look... "We'll be able to use these shades!" he said. "I did an analysis of those TVTrons we defeated earlier. I think we can use these shades to block their mind control ray."

"You're right. That sure would be useful," I said.

"Of course, I haven't been able to actually test them," Elvin said.

"Yes, well, that would make things too easy," I said.

"What's wrong with being too easy?" Zenna asked.

"It was a joke, Zen," I said as I sat in the pilot's seat.

"Oh. It wasn't a very good one."

"My job is to fly, not make good jokes." I said.

"That's for sure," SC, Zenna, Elvin and the princess all said. I took that as a good sign that my team and the princess were in sync.

"SC, are we cleared for takeoff?" I asked.

"Kappa has first clearance; you may follow them in one minute."

"Okay, people, let's get this over with and bring our guys home."

"Be safe and good luck," GiS called over our speaker.

I watched Kappa's shuttle take off. I took a deep breath. I powered up my shuttle. I exhaled and took off.

Chapter 18

WE WERE WITHIN VISUAL RANGE of the Explorer in minutes. It was still sitting there lifeless, but the strange thing was the landing bay doors were open — wide open.

"Lifeless and inviting is not a good combo," I said over the speaker so everybody could hear.

"They may have just not bothered to close the bay doors," Kymm suggested from her shuttle.

"I may not be that old, but I wasn't born yesterday either," I said. "I'm smart enough to know that if something looks too good to be true, it probably is."

"Yeah, well we don't have much choice," Kymm said. "We'll go in first and check it out."

"But my group has the experience," I said.

"But we're better rested," Kymm said. "Plus, with my computer-aided eyes, I can land under less than optimal conditions."

"She's right," SC, K-999 and GiS all said at once.

I looked at the princess. "As long as we get in to save our people I don't care who goes in first," she said.

"Okay, Kymm, we'll back you up."

"Smartest thing you've said in years," Kymm said over the speaker.

I turned and watched her shuttle head toward the Explorer. The shuttle flew into the Explorer and out of our sight.

"We're in," Kymm said over the speaker. "So far it's nice and quiet."

"The Explorer currently has life support up and working," I heard K-999 say over the comm.

That didn't sound right. It sounded too easy.

"Uh oh," Kymm called over the comm. "The lift door just opened. There have to be dozens of TVTrons pouring out of it."

"Are you on the left or right of the lift?" I asked over the comm.

"Ah, the left," Kymm said. "Why?"

"How many meters away are you?"

"Two hundred twenty-seven. I repeat why?"

I pushed my throttle down. I went shooting toward the Explorer at break-neck speed.

"What are you doing?" Elvin shouted.

"Landing on the Explorer," I said.

"You're going too fast!" Elvin shouted louder. "You can't control the landing..."

I looked at the princess. She gave me a little wink. That made me feel good. I ignored Elvin and kept zooming toward the Explorer...

"Uh, Baxter," GiS called from the Searcher, sounding much calmer than I know he felt. "What in Buck Roger's name are you doing?"

"I'm landing..." I said as we raced closer and closer to Explorer.

"At that speed you'll take out half the shuttle bay..." GiS said over the speaker.

"Exactly!"

"Humans, I let them go on one mission without me," GiS muttered.

Elvin looked at his console. "We'll be inside in ten tics..."

"Great. Kymm, you and your crew stay in your shuttle," I called over the comm.

"No problem..."

If this was going to work, I was going to have to time it just right. I was good, I knew that; but I was also going to have to be lucky.

As we were about at the bay door I eased off the throttle just enough. We cleared the door to the shuttle bay.

"We're in!" Elvin shouted, though it was fairly obvious.

I jammed on the air brakes. The shuttle started to screech and slow, but of course it didn't stop. I was counting on that fact to help us. We slid past Kymm's shuttle right toward the oncoming TVTrons.

The force of the shuttle's collision took out the lead TVTrons.

"You're using the shuttle like a giant bowling ball," Zenna said.

It was an interesting and surprisingly accurate observation.

I jerked the shuttle quickly to the right. The sudden action caused the shuttle to spin around in a circle. While we spun we took out more and more TVTrons. Of course we were also heading toward the shuttle bay wall. Spinning as we were I could only catch a glance of the wall when we faced it. But each time I caught a glimpse, it was closer and closer. My goal was to not only take out as many TVTrons as I could but to hit the wall with the shuttle's tail. That way I would at least be able to fly the shuttle out of here and then Kymm could tow us home.

"Brace for impact," I called to my crew.

"I've been braced since we came in here," Elvin said.

"I was braced before that," Zenna said.

"You are never boring, Baxter Moon," was all the princess said.

I jammed on brakes with all my might. We spun completely around a couple more times, taking out many TVTrons before we finally crashed into the far wall.

The crash was jolting but not deadly. After a couple of tics my brain stopped wiggling around in my skull.

I turned to the princess and my crew. "Are you all okay?"

"Not nearly as hurt I as thought I would be," Elvin said.

"That was kind of fun," Zenna said.

"Next time I drive," the princess said.

We looked on the bay landing floor. I had made quite a mess. There were huge skid and burn marks from the entry door to the wall. The floor was also littered with the broken remains of the TVTrons. It was quite a mess, a good mess.

"Good job," Kymm called over the comm. "You took them all out."

"SC, do you have any control of the ship?" K-999 asked over the comm.

"No, I do not," SC said bluntly.

Elvin looked at his console. "Interestingly, the TVTrons do have life support working at this level and the level above us."

"So they want us alive," the princess said.

"At least for now," I added.

"Just because they have it on now, doesn't mean they'll keep it on," K-999 growled. "I want the squads to disembark and make sure you all have your helmets, full air supply and energy rods."

"Plus, I've made three pairs of special glasses," Elvin said. "They should in theory block the TVTrons' hypnotic effect."

"Good job, Elvin," K-999 said. "Give a pair to Baxter, Zenna and Kymm."

"But…"

"They are the three best hand-to-hand fighters," K-999 said, before Elvin could say anything else.

Elvin handed a pair of the shades to Zenna.

"K-999 is right," she said to him. "I am much better in a fight than you are. But you are much smarter than me."

Elvin wasn't taking much consolation in that. He stalked over to me and handed me my glasses.

"Don't worry, Elvin, you did your part creating these. I bet they save the day."

"Just once I'd like to be the one who saves the day," he said.

"We all must do our parts." The princess said.

I slid the glasses onto my forehead. I positioned them down over my eyes. Everything looked slightly darker but not much different.

"I made them so they wouldn't filter out light," Elvin said. "Just the specific wavelength the TVTrons broadcast over."

I patted him on the shoulder. "Nice job, Elvin."

We got out of our shuttle, weapons ready. But there were no more TVTrons (besides the smashed ones) in sight. We met Kappa squad by the lift door, where Elvin gave Kymm her special shades. Watching the expression on Chriz's face, he was even less happy about this than Elvin. I was guessing that it wasn't so much that he didn't get shades or that Kymm did, it was more that I got shades.

Kymm smiled as she looked at the mess I had made out of the TVTrons. "Good job, Moon. You made the place a TVTron junk yard."

K-999 was all business. He sniffed the lift door. "SC, is the lift active?" he asked.

"Yes, surprisingly, it is. I have access to it."

"Now, that doesn't sound much like a trap," I said cynically.

"It does to me," Zenna said. She patted me on the shoulder. "Poor Baxter, you can be so naïve sometimes…"

"Well, if it is a trap, we don't have any other choice," Elvin said. He walked over to the door that led to the ladder. It was dangling on its hinges; apparently my shuttle crash had damaged it. He tossed the door to the floor. The bottom section of the ladder had been mangled.

"Oops," I said.

"That's okay, Baxter," K-999 said. "It's not like I could have taken the ladder anyhow…" K-999 paused for a tic. "SC, open the lift door please."

"As you wish."

The door slid open.

We all aimed our energy weapons at the lift. It was empty. K-999 sniffed the air and stepped on to the lift. He turned to us.

"Come on, squads, let's get this over with."

We all joined K-999 on the lift. The door shut and lift started to rise.

"I assume you want to go to the conference room on the first floor," SC said.

"Very good, SC," I said.

"Are there still life signs there?" K-999 asked.

"Yes, sixteen human and sixteen Aquarian."

The lift stopped. We all pointed out weapons at the door. The door slid open to reveal a huge conference room. Sure enough, there was a group of adult humans sitting on one side of a long table and a group of adult Aquarians sitting across from them. None of them were looking at each other. Each of them were concentrating on a TVTron sitting on the table in front of them.

"Well, at least we came to right place," K-999 said.

Chapter 19

A S WE ENTERED THE CONFERENCE ROOM, none of the humans, Aquarians or TVTrons paid any attention to us. The walls of the conference room were giant display screens filled with static.

"This is weird," I said looking at the static. "They don't seem to care that we are here..."

"Greetings, young and annoying beings, I am UHF-1," a voice said from the wall display screens.

We all looked up at the screens. The static became clearer and clearer until it was replaced with the image of a TVTron. This TVTron looked much like the others except it had the image of human face on its screen. It appeared to be a male with a big smile and bigger eyes. He reminded me of a deranged talk show host of the past.

The princess glared at the screen. "I want my people back!"

"Not going to happen," UHF-1 said.

"That's what you think!" the princess said. She aimed her energy rod. The TVTrons were positioned in two straight lines on the table. The princess fired. Her first shot ripped through one TVTron, then another, then another, then another, until the first row was destroyed. The princess aimed and fired at the second row. Once again her one shot channeled through each of the TVTrons, destroying them.

The princess turned defiantly toward the screen. "I took out all your creatures in two shots!"

UHF-1 yawned. "Yes, bully for you," he said. "Excellent shot! I'm sure our viewers will be pleased."

"Your viewers?" I said.

"Yes," UHF-1 said. "When we first encountered your people we were quite content with having you watch us. But now we have decided it is much more entertaining to watch you. You see, we have evolved from entertainers to producers and consumers."

"I don't know if that can really be classified as evolving," Elvin said.

UHF-1 ignored him. "You see, we have learned from your history that wars are great attention grabbers and score well in the ratings. So we have decided to start a war between Earth and Aqua."

"Not going to happen," the princess said. "We've destroyed your drones and now we will return to our planets and tell our people the truth!"

The face on UHF-1's screen just smiled. I didn't like that smile one little iota.

"I will give you that; you have destroyed my drones, as you call them. The superduper thing is, the drones had already served their purpose."

"Uh oh," I said. "I don't like the tone of that..."

"As you will soon see, much to the joy and anticipation of our audience, the drones no longer entertain, they reprogram," UHF-1 said.

As the UHF-1 finished saying that, all the people at the table stood up and turned to us.

"We will not return to our planets," they said in one voice. One very creepy, sort of robotic voice.

We slowly backed up.

"We can't shoot our own people," Kymm said.

"We could stun them and have Zenna carry them to our shuttles," Chriz suggested.

"Yes, that might work," UHF-1 said. "It would certainly make for exciting, almost nerve-tingling viewing!"

A group of our people and Aquarians were slowly moving toward us. We opened up fire on them. The jolts from our energy rods sent them staggering backwards maybe a step. They shuddered, then began moving forward again.

"We found we could not only program you organics but we can also increase your strength and physical endurance," UHF-1 said. "They will happily ignore your low-powered energy-stun blasts. You would have to use deadly power to stop them."

"We can't use deadly power on our own people," the princess said. "Well, maybe we could on humans, but certainly not on mine."

I had to give the princess some credit. She always put her people first. Of course she needed to work on her interplanetary relation skills, but I guess that would come with time.

"Even if we could, we couldn't," K-999 said. "These energy rods have stun-only modes."

I had to give K-999 his kudos. No matter what the situation he always had his good old canine sensibility about him. (Unless of course the situation involved chasing bunnies or an old sock for him to play with.)

"I'll slow them down," Zenna said. She leapt forward toward the swarming artificial zombies. "I don't want to hurt you, but I must stop you."

Zenna grabbed a human diplomat who was leading the crowd. He was a short bearded man who must have been in his forties. The man reacted by hitting Zenna with an uppercut to her chin. The blow was surprisingly effective. It sent Zenna reeling back a couple of steps.

Two other attackers, a skinny Aquarian man and an older human woman leapt forward and dragged Zenna to the ground. Zenna struggled to break free, but she couldn't.

"We found we can also stimulate an area in the brain to make you stronger," UHF-1 said proudly. "As you can see, our R&D boys have been working hand in hand with our producers to give our audiences a complete experience."

"Fall back into the lift," K-999 ordered.

"But, Zenna," Elvin said.

"Fall back," K-999 barked.

Everybody but Elvin moved quickly to the lift. When I saw that Elvin was just standing there staring helplessly at his struggling sister, I moved toward him. He may not have been the bravest guy in the room but he didn't want let his sister down. The thing is, action wasn't Elvin's strong point. He was a thinking kind of guy. Getting himself captured wasn't going to help anybody.

"Come on, Elvin," I said. "You won't be any good to Zen if you get caught."

Elvin still didn't budge. A mob of programmed zombies was staggering toward us. I yanked Elvin toward the lift. At first he resisted, just staring at Zenna. Finally, his survival instinct kicked in.

"You're right," he said, reluctantly.

We turned and rushed into the lift. The door to the lift closed right behind us, just a few tics before the programmed zombies slammed into it.

We all breathed a little sigh of relief from the lift. Of course it was only a very little sigh as our planet mates were on the other side pounding at the door.

"Now what?" Chriz asked.

"We head back to the Searcher, then to Earth to warn them," K-999 said.

"No!" the princess and Elvin both said.

"If we get captured, then…"

"Then, Lobi and GiS will have to go warn Earth and Aqua without us," I said.

"But without the princess, Aqua may not believe it," K-999 insisted.

Elvin pulled out his communication device/mini-computer. He entered in some calculations. "I think I can use SC to send some feedback over the signal the TVTrons used to control our people. I think I can break their hold."

"You think?" K-999 said. "I need more than a hunch…"

The TVTron-made zombies started pounding loudly on the lift door.

"I can't be certain," Elvin said. "I haven't run any simulations. But it's kind of like what I did to the bots earlier."

"SC, what do you think?" I asked.

"E=MC squared. The shortest distance between two points is a straight line. What goes up must come down unless it breaks free from the gravitational attraction of the planet. Of course some people don't think I technically think."

Okay, I wasn't sure if it was me or not, but SC seemed to be getting stranger and stranger. I didn't know if it was some form of TVTron attack on him or the stress from defending us against the attack.

"What do you think about Elvin's plan?"

"Oh, it might work."

"Can you be more specific?" I asked.

"Yes."

"Will you please be more specific?"

"Of course. I deduce there is a 48 percent chance of success," SC said.

"Actually, I calculate it's more like 46.89 percent," Elvin said.

"I was giving you the benefit of the doubt," SC said.

"Thanks," Elvin said. "I found the frequency, but we don't have a way of delivering it to the victims. We're being blocked from computer access."

"That is correct," SC said.

"Then we have a problem," K-999 said.

"Maybe not," Chriz said. "We have the energy rods. Sound is just another form of energy."

Elvin's eyes lit up. "I can modify the energy rods!" he said. He pulled up his shirt just a bit to unveil the utility belt he wore around his waist. He pulled out a tool that looked like a four-prong tuning folk with circuits on the tips. "I actually experimented with this once, back a few years ago, for an extra credit project."

Elvin popped open the base of his energy rod to reveal the circuits under the handle. He hooked up the energy rod to his wrist scanner and started tweaking the rod by waving the fork-shaped tool over it in different directions at different speeds. As he moved the freaky fork back and forth, the energy rod made a series of high-pitched noises. "I knew this would come in handy someday!" he said proudly. Making some adjustments on the fork with his fingers, he then used it to tweak another energy rod setting while he looked at the screen on his wrist scanner. He smiled.

"That should do it!" he said happily.

"That fast?" K-999 said.

"Hey, when you're a geek, you're a geek," Elvin said.

No truer words had ever been spoken.

"Are you sure it works?" K-999 asked.

"As sure as I can be, without spending weeks on simulations."

Okay, it wasn't exactly a ringing endorsement, but it was good enough for me. After all, I didn't see a whole lot of other choices here. Something had to be done and fast. I had learned to trust the instincts of my crew.

I took the energy rod from Elvin.

"I'll test it out," I said.

Princess Amana stepped toward us. She handed Elvin her power rod. "Convert mine too," she ordered. "Baxter will need backup."

Elvin took the princess's energy rod and popped the handle open. The look on his face could only be described as pure joy. He was helping the cause by doing something he was good at and loved doing. I guess that's about all a person, any person, can ask out of life.

"I should have this one converted even quicker than Baxter's," he said with unmitigated glee. "Once you do this once, it's easy."

"Good," I told him. "The rest of you should keep your weapons as is. Just in case we run into more bots or TVTrons. The two of us should be able to unzap the brains of all our people."

K-999 had a worried look on his face. You know a dog is really worried when you can tell by just looking at him.

"Don't worry, Commander," I said to him, "this is going work."

"Well, it better," K-999 said, "because I don't see a lot of other options besides putting our tails between our legs and running."

Elvin finished making the modifications on the princess's energy rod. He handed it to her with a big grin.

"I've increased the area and effective range of the rod," he said. "You don't even have to hit your target. It should work on any target within a three meter area."

The princess shook the rod up and down in her hand. "It feels exactly the same," she said.

"As well it should," Elvin said.

The princess and I exchanged glances. We were both ready to rescue our people from the control of the TVTrons. I winked at her. She winked back. I leaned over and gave her a kiss.

"What was that for?" the princess asked.

"Just in case," I said.

"In case?"

"On the off chance we don't survive, now I'll have no regrets," I told her.

Now Kymm chimed in. "I hate to break up this love fest, but what about me? With my bionic eye I'm at the very least as good a shot as anybody here."

I was actually surprised Kymm had taken so long to speak her piece. She was a pilot like I was. She wasn't used to sitting in the back. I was going to have to appeal to her pilot's personality to get out of this smoothly.

"We can't risk both our pilots out there," I said. "If something happens to me, it will be up to you to get everybody back to the Searcher and then back to Earth."

Kymm just looked at me for a tic or two. On some level she knew I was only saying what I said to make her happy. On another level though she knew it made sense. Of course her pride would kick in.

"It's not easy being me," she said, "being the best pilot and the best shot."

"Yes, it must be a terrible burden to bear," Chriz said, not being able to resist sucking up.

"Oh, yes, lucky for all of us you are such a wise and wonderful person," I said.

Kymm shot me a grin. "Damn straight," she said.

K-999 cleared his throat, subtly. Which isn't easy to do if you're a dog. "Uh, folks, we have a mission to do," he said.

Not that any of us could have forgotten that with the constant pounding and moaning on the door. But he was right. The prepping and the ego boosting were done. It was time for action.

"Okay SC, open the door," I ordered.

"Are you sure?" SC said. "I have some access to the Explorer's cameras and I see that there are currently ten zombies leaning on the door. If the modified weapon does not work you will all quickly be taken captive."

I thought for a minute. SC certainly had a good point. If this didn't work then we'd be making ourselves easy to capture with no backup plan in place.

"We are on an elevator and the zombies aren't going anywhere," Kymm said. "We can go down to the bay area, just far enough from the action so we can help or retreat."

We all looked at each other and nodded.

"I'm lowering the lift now," SC said.

There was silence on the way down. The trip couldn't have taken a minute, but it seemed longer. I guess that's why people make small talk; it helps make time pass quicker. Only in this case the situation was too big for small talk.

The lift stopped.

"We have reached the bay," SC announced. "I have scanned the area. There are no hostiles present."

K-999 led Kymm, Chriz and Elvin off the lift. Before Kymm walked off, she turned to me. "Good luck," she said.

I gave her a little salute. "When you're good you don't need luck," I said as the door closed.

"You better hope for all the luck you can get," I heard Kymm yell through the door as we started our way back up.

The trip up to the conference room went a lot faster than the trip down. The princess and I didn't say anything to each other. After all, there wasn't anything that needed to be said. We knew what we had to do.

"We have arrived," SC said.

"Open the door on three."

The princess and I both pointed our rods at the door.

"Why do you humans always pick three? Why not two or five?" SC asked.

"Tradition," I said.

"Yes, you are creatures of habit."

"Can we get back to the business at hand, SC?"

"I am a very powerful mega super computer. I can open a door and still have a conversation about human idiosyncrasies."

"Maybe so, but the princess and I need to concentrate," I said.

"Ah yes, good point. I am ready at your command."

"Thanks, one, two, open the door."

The door receded into the wall. The sudden move caught the zombies who had been pounding on the door totally off guard. They weren't used to us making it so easy on them. The lead zombies who were leaning on the door fell into the elevator.

The princess and I both aimed our weapons and fired at them. The weapons made a strange buzzing noise, but nothing else seemed to happen. The zombies who were on the ground suddenly stopped trying to get back to their feet. Their eyes which had been glazed over in a mental fog suddenly cleared. They were confused about what had happened, but it looked like they were once again in control of their actions.

I took this as a sign that our little tweaked devices were working. I quickly aimed and fired at the second group that had been standing right outside the entrance but weren't leaning on the doors. They had started to lurch into the lift. A split second after I fired they stopped. They shook their heads. Their eyes cleared. They, like the others, were still dazed but they were no longer dangerous. I smiled and pushed my way past them into the conference room. The princess followed close behind.

"You take your people and I will take my people," she said.

"Too complicated, Your Highness. You take the right side of the room, I'll take the left."

"Simple but effective," she said.

"The story of my life."

I wanted to move fast. Even though our plan seemed to be working, I knew we had to execute it fast before the TVTrons had a chance to react. A couple other zombies came at me. I blasted them. (Well, actually I sound-waved them, but blasting sounds cooler.) They instantly stopped coming at me.

I ran toward the spot where four zombies had Zenna pinned to the wall. I had to give Zen credit. She was still fighting.

"I'll never give up," Zenna shouted.

I aimed in the middle of the four of them. My rod made the strange buzzing sound. The four of them instantly stopped struggling with Zenna and released their grip on her.

"Thanks," Zenna called to me as I ran by.

"Since your weapons work, I told the others to join us on this floor," SC said over my communicator.

"That's kind of not your place," I said as I continued to run. "I thought your job was just to give information, not make decisions."

"My job is to be efficient," SC said. "This is the most efficient way. Doing it my way means you can save at least thirty tics!"

I was too busy to argue. Besides I've learned that arguing with a super computer is even more futile than arguing with Elvin. Above and beyond that, I had to admit SC had a point.

I threw myself onto the long table that traversed the room. I slid down the table, aiming my rod to the left and firing away as fast as my hand could squeeze the trigger. I figured this would give me great coverage of the left side of the room. After a few tics I had slid across a good portion of the table. By the time my momentum gave out I was three-quarters of the way down the table. I aimed my rod up and fired a couple more times, just to make sure I got everybody on my side.

I sat up and looked around. All the zombies that had been on the left side of the room were now standing there shaking their heads. I looked to my right. All the zombies on the right were also returning to normal. The princess had managed to get her side cleared without sliding on the table.

I hopped off the table and over to the princess. "Nice job," I said.

"When you are as accurate with a power rod as I am, you don't need to be flashy," she said with a superior smile.

"Let's get our ambassadors and our people out of here," I said.

I never met our ambassador, but he was still easy to pick out from the crowd, especially now that the crowd wasn't trying to kill us. He was a balding, middle-aged man with a big stomach, wearing a fancy, gold dress uniform with stars running up and down his sleeves and his pant legs. I of course couldn't see it but I was betting his underwear had stars on it also.

"Ambassador?" I said as I ran up to him.

"Yes, I am Ambassador W.G. Plant. You may address me as Your Excellency," he said very dignified. "Who are you? Why are you here? Where is here?"

"The who is easy, I'm Baxter Moon, Galactic Scout Second Class," I said. "We're on the Explorer. The why is a bit harder to explain." I pointed to the lift. "I suggest I explain it on the way out of here."

Ambassador Plant, who was obviously still a little dazed and confused, nodded. "Yes, I'm not sure why, but I totally agree with you."

"Everybody on the lift now!" I shouted. "Let's move it, people!"

We took the lift down to the bay area. We entered the bay with our weapons ready, but met with no resistance either from the TVTrons or any of the machines on Explorer. We scanned the bay for some sort of hostile activity but it was calm.

"It's quiet. Too quiet," Elvin said. He paused for a tic. "I just love saying that!" he said.

"I guess we've given them enough of beating," Kymm said.

K-999 took a quick head count. There were thirty-two politicians, sixteen from Earth and sixteen from Aqua. "We need to split up." K-999 pointed with his nose to Kymm's ship. "The ones from Earth will go with Cadet Clark."

Kymm saluted to Ambassador Plant. "I'm sure you and your people will find the ride on my shuttle back to the Searcher acceptable," she said.

The ambassador gave Kymm a polite bow. "I am sure my staff and I will find the ride more than acceptable," he said.

K-999 pointed to my shuttle, leaning against the wall. "The Aquarians will ride with Scout Moon."

A very formal looking woman with light blue hair done up in a bun looked at my beat-up shuttle. She shook her head. "Why do the Earthlings get the better shuttle?"

The princess spoke for K-999. "Ambassador Marga," she said sternly, "I assure you Baxter Moon is a fine pilot. We could not be in better hands."

Ambassador Marga looked at my shuttle, she looked back at me, then back at the shuttle. Finally her gaze met the princess's gaze. She bowed deeply. You could see she knew the princess and that she didn't have the chance of a snow ball on the sun of winning this one.

"I am not one to argue with my princess," she said.

"Good," the princess said. She pointed to my shuttle. "I suggest we board before the TVTrons have more time to counteract our moves."

"Yes, Your Highness," the entire Aquarian delegation said.

The two groups split up. Kymm, her crew and the Earthlings to her shuttle; my crew, the Aquarians and I to my shuttle.

"Thanks for the compliment, Your Highness," I said.

"I had to do it to reassure my people," she said. She gave me a little wink. "You may call me Princess." I took that as a good sign.

Chapter 20

I LED MY TEAM AND THE AQUARIANS into my shuttle. To be on the safe side, I entered with two energy weapons ready. This way I could handle either TVTrons or any leftover zombies that we didn't know about. The shuttle was empty, though. I wasn't sure if the TVTrons had given up or were prepping for a new attack. Whatever, I decided it was best not to worry about it. Like GiS would always harp, worrying doesn't help; if you're prepared you don't have to worry. I sort of understood that now. I was well trained and fast on my feet. I was prepared for anything the TVTrons could muster.

SC had the shuttle ready for us. The extra passenger seats were up and ready. I had to give SC credit. He might have been acting a bit odd, but he was also making good choices.

"The quicker you take your seats, the quicker we'll be out of here," I said to the Aquarian party. "Please buckle your harnesses."

They still weren't exactly clear what had happened, but they knew it wasn't pleasant and none of them wanted to hang around any longer. They hastily grabbed seats and sat down.

I looked at my crew. They were already at their stations preparing for takeoff. I couldn't help being proud.

I headed to the pilot's seat. I sat down and buckled myself in. This was going to be a rocky flight, but I didn't want to say that.

The princess sat next to me and buckled in. She gave me a forced grin. "I have faith in you, Baxter, but this is going to be tricky, even for you."

I couldn't blame her for being scared. My shuttle didn't look like it could fly across the street, much less across space. It wasn't going to be easy to fly. Yet I knew my shuttle, my crew and I could do this.

"Tricky is my middle name," I said.

"What an odd name"

"It was a joke, princess."

"Oh, not a very good one."

"You just don't get Earth humor."

The princess just looked at me. "True, I studied your greatest Earth comics — the Six Stooges — and I barely smiled... I found them to be not at all entertaining."

"Don't worry, princess, you'll grow to appreciate my humor." I told her.

"I hate to interrupt the sparkling banter," Kymm called from her shuttle. "But we have to hightail it out of here. Since my shuttle's still in good shape, I should lead the way out."

"I won't argue with you there, Kymm," I said.

"Once you clear the Explorer I'll give you a tow back to the Searcher. Then we're back to good old terra firma."

"Once again I won't argue," I said.

I looked over at Kymm in her shuttle and gave her a formal salute. She returned the salute with a crisp salute of her own. She fired up her shuttle and easily steered it out of the Explorer.

Now it was my turn. I fired up my engine. It complained a bit and rumbled a bit more, but it did eventually spring, well at least crawl, to life.

I touched the accelerator just enough to ease us away from the wall. We wobbled forward.

"Are you sure this ship will hold together?" Ambassador Marga asked.

"Of course he is!" Princess Amana said. Turning to me she said, "You are sure. Right, Baxter?"

"Of course I am!" I said, trying to sound more confident than I felt.

I eased the shuttle forward. It made a slight creaking noise when it pulled away from the wall. The noise caused the entire Aquarian delegation to gasp.

"Nothing to worry about," I said loudly so everybody could hear.

I nudged the control stick forward. The shuttle started to roll toward the bay door. We were a little off center so I realigned her a bit. The handling wasn't as precise as it normally was but it was still acceptable. I checked my radar. Kymm had cleared the Explorer and was now hovering 500 meters above it. She was in position to catch us should we start to plummet once we made our exit. Apparently Kymm had about as much confidence as the Aquarians. I checked my boosters and engines. They were both still at 70 percent so we would have enough power. The question was, how much would I be able to control the shuttle in gravityless space?

We moved forward. The shuttle seemed fairly stable, which made me reasonably confident. We cleared the opening. We were back in space, but for once in my life I wasn't that thrilled to be there. My shuttle had taken a lot of damage in my crash landing, but I hoped it still had enough left in it to make the trip back to the Searcher.

I pushed the acceleration button. "Come on baby! Let's go!" I coaxed.

The shuttled rocked forward.

"Does talking to it help?" the princess asked.

"It doesn't hurt," I said.

I looked at my meters. Everything looked okay. Not great, but at least I should have enough power to make the quick trip over.

I pulled back on the control stick. The shuttle pulled up. It didn't have the instant response it normally had but it was still good enough. We started to climb and pull away from the Explorer.

I pushed the throttle forward and headed toward the Searcher. The ship was shaky but controllable.

"Uh oh," Elvin said.

"What? I don't like Uh oh," I said.

"We're leaking fluids!"

"Which ones?" I asked.

Elvin looked at his console. "It would be easier to list all the ones that aren't leaking." Elvin squinted at his console. "Our engines and controls will be dead, in three, two, one, now."

The shuttle jerked, sputtered, only we didn't stop. In fact our momentum kept sending us forward, but only now I had even less (actually no) control. We were blasting forward out of control. We were like a bullet, a big ten-ton bullet. That's the thing about flying in space, once you get moving forward you actually need your reverse thrusters to slow you down. Or else you keep going either forever or until you hit something. In this case it would be the latter and the something would be the Searcher.

"Baxter, you're going way too fast," Kymm called from her ship. Just in case I hadn't noticed. "You have to take control of your ship."

"Elvin, you got to be able to give me reverse thrusters," I pleaded.

Elvin studied his console. Zenna got out of her chair and moved over next to Elvin. They both stared at the console. Elvin pointed to the screen. "If we reroute this and this we should get reverse thrusters back online."

"Baxter, you're coming in too fast," GiS said. "I can only assume you've lost your reverse thrusters and not your mind."

"Nice to have you back in communication," I said. "And that your instincts are just as keen as ever."

"SC, why haven't you been keeping us all informed?" K-999 asked.

"I'm sorry, K-999, but TVTrons are constantly attempting to infect us with a virus. It has put me a bit under the chips. I can still function, but it takes much of my capacity to keep them from overwhelming me. I have fought off over a million attempts in the last nanosecond alone."

I looked at the screen. We were getting closer and closer to the Searcher. I looked back at Elvin and Zenna. "How you guys coming?"

"Ah, fine," Elvin said. He moved his fingers over the console. "You have reverse thrusters now!"

We were going pretty fast. I didn't want to slam on the reverse thrusters, but I also didn't want to slam into the Searcher. I hit the reverse thrusters. We started to slow, but we were still heading pretty quickly toward Searcher.

"Kymm, I'm going to need you," I said.

"I'm right above you," Kymm called over the comm. "I'm locking on in three tics. Prepare your passengers."

"You can't, Kymm. Locking on to us at this speed could drag your shuttle crashing into the Searcher with us," I shouted.

"That's why she's not going to lock on," Chriz said over the comm. "I've rigged the tractor beam so it will throw a tractor pulse cushion around you. It will stop you but it won't be connected to us. It will be like we've thrown a big soft cushy pillow around you."

"Wow, what a great idea," Elvin said. I detected a hint of jealousy in his voice.

"Buckle up and hold on, everybody," I called. "This is going to be rough."

Shuttles in space were meant to come to nice gradual stops. They weren't really built to be going from 17,000 kilometers per hour to zero in under a tic, but in this case we didn't have any choice. The instant stop would beat a next instant crash.

The shuttle slammed to a complete stop. All of us on board jerked forward. It wasn't smooth by any means, but it certainly beat crashing.

"Gotcha!" Kymm said.

"Okay, maybe not a really soft pillow," Chriz said.

"Nice shot," I told her. "Now guide us in."

I put my hands up on my head and relaxed. After all there was nothing I could do but sit back and relax.

"You seem very confident," Princess Amana said to Kymm over the comm.

"I learned by watching him," Kymm called. "You're going to be fine."

Within minutes we were safely docked on the Searcher.

Chapter 21

WE WERE ALL ECSTATIC WHEN WE got off our shuttles. We had done it! We had saved the diplomats. Now we just needed to warp to Earth and tell them what had happened. War would be avoided and all would be saved.

Of course it couldn't be that easy. Could it?

K-999 confirmed our arrival to GiS. "We are all aboard. Fire up the light-speed engines and let's get out of here."

"We have a problem," GiS said.

No, of course it couldn't be that easy.

"I need everybody to the command center stat," GiS said.

"I demand to know what's going on!" Ambassador Plant said.

"I also demand to know!" Ambassador Marga said.

"There is a TVTron mothership-pyramid coming at us," GiS said curtly.

I turned to the ambassadors. "You had to ask."

We all hurried to the command center.

———◆———

Sure enough, when we reached the command center, there on main view screen heading right for us was a huge reflective-silver giant pyramid with an old-fashioned satellite antenna on top of each of its three base points. GiS was standing in the middle of the room nervously scratching his head with his foot.

"So that's a TVTron mothership-pyramid," Elvin said.

"That is correct," SC said.

"Just once why can't something be simple…," I sighed. Sure, it wasn't professional to sigh, but this was a matter worth sighing over.

"It's locked on to me with a tractor beam," SC said.

"Fire up the light-speed engines and get out of here!" Ambassador Marga ordered.

"Yes, fire them up!" Ambassador Plant reordered.

GiS turned to them. "The engines take an hour to come online."

Ambassador Plant looked at the TVTron Pyramid in the view screen. It certainly was an impressive sight. He pointed at the screen. "But we don't have an hour!"

"Hence the problem," GiS said.

UHF-1 appeared on our view screen. It was smiling.

"Thank you for such a rousing attempted escape, I am sure our viewers will enjoy it. Still we can not let you back to your planet to warn them. We need more action. We crave it. We long for it. We live for it."

"You have to stop them!" both ambassadors said at the same time.

"Yes, I know," GiS said.

The Searcher opened up fire with two of its laser cannons at the TVTron pyramid. The shots glanced harmlessly off the pyramid's sides.

"Why don't you blast them out of the sky!? Nuke 'em!" Ambassador Marga shouted.

"Our ship is not carrying heavy weapons," GiS said. "Remember our deal?"

"Oh that's right," Ambassador Marga said. "We probably should have trusted each other more..." She stopped to think for a tic. "Wait a minute, you shouldn't even have small weapons!"

"We brought them online just to fight some TVTron attack ships," Zenna said.

Two giant robotic crane arms rolled out of the side of the pyramid. Another popped out of the bottom. Though we were still hundreds of kilometers away, we could see the claws and arms with our naked eyes.

One of the Aquarians pointed to the claws on the screen. "They are going to rip us apart!"

UHF-1's voice came in over our comm system. "We find viewers savor having ships ripped apart far longer than they do if we simply blow them up with fast, boring lasers or missiles."

This didn't look good at all. We were being drawn closer and closer to the claws of death — literally.

"One of your shuttles could ram the pyramid," one of the Aquarians, a short man with no eyebrows and green hair suggested. "That would allow us to escape and to warn our planets."

Elvin did a few calculations on a console. "One of our shuttles ramming the pyramid wouldn't do enough damage to stop it." He did a few more calculations. "Even if we hit it with both our shuttles, we still wouldn't stop it."

The princess turned to me. "Baxter, do something," she said. It wasn't an order. It wasn't a request. It was a statement.

A simple statement, yet somehow it made me feel good. The princess wasn't just hoping I would think of something to save the day, she knew I would.

I had to think and I had to think hard. We needed a big weapon and we needed it fast.

"Can we radio back to our planets and tell them the situation? At least we can avoid war," one of the aids suggested.

Both ambassadors shook their heads no. "All communication is being blacked out." The two ambassadors looked at each other.

"We have to learn to trust each other more," Plant said.

"I agree," Marga said.

The two exchanged grins. They shook hands. It would have been a nice moment if we weren't all about to die.

"We should have gotten more done on the Explorer," Plant said.

Then it hit me. Proving once again you never know where inspiration will spring from. "The Explorer!" I said.

Chriz turned to me. "No, Moon, we're on the Searcher, try to stick with the program."

"I know where we are, but we can use the Explorer. We can ram the mothership-pyramid with the Explorer!"

Ambassador Plant looked at me. "Son, the Explorer is a 20-billion-international-dollar piece of equipment. We can't use it as a giant rock."

Everybody in the room just looked at him. The ambassador sank back. "Sorry, sometimes I do politics first and think second."

Ambassador Marga put her hand on his shoulder. "Our ship has already been destroyed, so now our planets will share an even stronger common bond."

"Yes, good point," Plant said.

Of course it would be a moot point if we couldn't pull this off. I turned to my team.

"Do we have any access to Explorer?"

"We're too far away," Chriz said.

"That is correct," SC said. "At this distance and under the current situation I can access the levels of their systems but not override them."

"Let's boost our signal."

Lobi, Elvin and Chriz started kicking around ideas.

"We could super charge SC."

"We could override the Explorer's override controls…"

That's the thing about super-brains, they may be super smart but sometimes they look for a complicated answer when the simple will do. By the time they finished sifting through all the options we'd be dead.

"We could…."

"We don't need a lot of control. We just need to be able to ram it into a giant mothership," I said.

The three of them looked at each other.

"We could send a single encoded-in-subspace command that basically says, fire up your engines and go this way," Lobi said.

"Yes, if we keep the beam tight enough we could get through to them. They wouldn't even notice."

"How long would that take?" Kymm asked.

"One hour, two tops," Lobi said.

I looked at the view screen. The TVTron ship wasn't coming at us at high speed (I guess they wanted to build tension) but it still didn't look like we had an hour.

"How long do we have until they reach us?" I asked.

"Five minutes," SC said. "Six tops if they want to drag it on a bit for their viewers."

"Then we need to send a transmission in four minutes," I said.

"But Baxter!" they all said at once.

"Come on guys. I know you always overestimate your estimates to make yourselves look good," I said.

"Yes, but not by a factor of twelve!" Lobi said.

"Well then work fast."

The three of them huddled together. They would come up with something. I knew they would, but I had to delay. Delaying was my specialty.

"SC, put me through to the UHF-1," I said.

"They may not be accepting calls," SC said.

I always prided myself as being creative and able to think fast on my feet. Now I had to put my money where my brain was. I needed an idea and fast.

"Tell them this will be a big ratings booster."

Okay, it wasn't the best idea. But it was a stall until I came up with something better. I knew I had something better in me.

UHF-1 appeared on our screen.

"Yes, what is it, humans?"

I had to play with his ego and his urge to entertain himself and his viewers at all costs. It came to me. We had to get him to play this up.

"So this is your big plan?" I taunted. "Crush us and then start a war between Earth and Aqua."

UHF-1 just looked at the screen. He crossed his robotic claw arms. "Yes, it is," he said defiantly. He stuck a little electronic tongue out at me. "I thought you said this would help boost our ratings…"

"Yeah, I did. It still amazes me that this is the best show you could up with," I said, just stalling for time.

UHF-1 pointed at the screen with a claw. "I admit we didn't spend a lot of time in developing the concept. We're on a limited budget. We prefer to use our resources on equipment. We figure a good story will write itself. What's your point, human? I'm sorry if you don't like the way we're killing you. But these are tough financial times so hard choices have to be made."

Time was running out. I needed to come up with something to stall them. And I needed it about five minutes ago. An idea popped into my head. It wasn't the greatest idea of all time. It probably wasn't even in the top hundred of great ideas of all time, but it was all I had. So I went with it.

"You know what fans really love?" I paused to build suspense and give us more time.

UHF-1 let out a little sigh. "I'll bite. What would the fans love?"

"A big chase scene. You can't beat a good chase scene for building dramatic tension."

UHF-1 looked into the screen. He was thinking. I could see it in his computer generated little beady eyes.

"Yes, that is true, that is why we let you escape from your first ship," UHF-1 said.

"True, but that was kind of boring. Why not release us from your tracker beam and chase us around a bit. Clacking your giant claws and such. The viewers will eat that up."

"You are just trying to delay," UHF-1 said. "You want to charge your engines and escape."

He was smarter than I thought. I don't know why I thought that since TVTrons had pretty much had us on the run the whole time.

"You know it will take us an hour to charge our engines. Correct?"

"Yes, that is correct."

"Then chase us around for a half hour before you crush us," I said.

"You wish to give yourselves more time to escape," UHF-1 said.

"Well, duh," I said. "We each get a little something. You get more footage and we get a chance."

There was silence on the other end — calculated silence.

"The tractor beam has been retracted," SC said.

"Move around," UHF-1 said. "You have fifteen of your minutes."

"Thanks," I said.

"Anything for the fans," UHF-1 said.

I slid my finger across my neck, giving my people the signal to cut the transmission. I turned to my team. "You guys have fourteen minutes to come up with something."

For the next ten minutes or so we ran around space with the TVTrons on our tail. They would get close enough to nip us but not to destroy us. As the clock ticked down I got impatient.

"We can tap into the Explorer's system," Lobi said, "but its main control computer is completely wiped. So we can't send it any control commands."

Finally, Kymm came with an idea. "Let's control it from here, via a remote."

Lobi and Elvin just looked at each other and smiled. They made a few calculations. "We can give you one shot," they said.

Zenna pulled out a spare shuttle control stick that she always kept nearby (don't ask). She quickly wired it into one of the Searcher's consoles. Lobi and Elvin made a few more alterations.

A small window appeared on the main view screen. "This is the view from the Explorer," Elvin said. "It's all you have to guide you while you steer."

I looked at Kymm. "Which one of us is going to steer this thing?"

She shook her head. "You're always better than me at games. I might have enhanced eye sight, but this is going to be more of a go-with-your-gut thing."

"Fine, I'll do it."

I looked at GiS who had been silent for longer than I have ever known him to be.

"You've been quiet. No chimp wisdom for me?"

GiS just shook his head. "No. I only impart my opinion when needed. You're doing well enough without me."

"You think I can handle this?" I said.

GiS just smiled. "Does it matter? You're our only chance."

I wasn't sure what to say to that.

GiS patted me on the shoulder with his foot. "You may not be the brightest cadet. You may not be the best pilot. You may not be the most ambitious."

"You're not building my confidence here, GiS..."

"Yet despite that, you're still our best hope. There's something about you, Baxter, that I can't put my fingers or toes on. Something we can't analyze. Somehow when the chips are down you always manage to make the right choice — do the right thing. It's something that can't be taught. It's something that can't be programmed into machines. It's something I doubt you even know you do."

I smiled. Not because GiS had just given me a compliment, but because this was the long winded GiS I knew.

"So what you're saying is, I guess, good..."

GiS raised an eyebrow. "I guess so. I like to think all the training I have given you does have some effect in the outcome. Maybe not on the guessing part, but on the other parts."

The princess and Chriz came running up to us with two of the ambassadors' staff, one from Earth and one from Aqua. "We've got some good news. These guys and I figured out how to supercharge the light-speed engines. We can have them online, fast. We can't travel long or far, but we can get out of here," Chriz said.

"Yes, we'll have it up it in three minutes," the princess said proudly. "We Aquarians have a knack for these things."

Even with the improvements, we were going to have to time this just right. But if we pulled it off, we'd be able to take out the TVTrons and get out of the way of the shock blast. War would be averted. Two worlds would be saved. Sure, a lot of things would have to go right. My timing was going to have to be near perfect. It was a lot to think about, so I figured it was better not to think about it. No need to put any extra pressure on myself.

Lobi made a couple of last minute calculations and adjustments. "We're ready to go!" he said.

Zenna handed me the control stick. I took a deep breath. "This is just like playing a video game," I said, trying to reinforce the idea to myself.

"True," Zenna said. "Only if you lose in this game you lose two whole worlds."

What could I say? Zenna always calls them like she sees them, for better or for worse.

I played with the control stick in my hand. It didn't quite feel like the one on my shuttle, but it was close enough. I took a deep breath. I took another deep breath.

I looked over at Elvin. He pointed at me. "We're online in three, two, one. We're live."

I looked at the TVTron Pyramid in the window. It was about 10,000 kilometers away from the Explorer. But I knew that distance would be covered in just a little more than a blink or two of the eye. I pushed the control stick forward. I could see the TVTron pyramid growing larger.

Kymm looked at me. "We can warp burst on your mark, Baxter."

The image of the pyramid grew on the screen. Still, it looked (or felt) like we were a little off. I tilted the stick to the left. I even tilted my body a bit. I don't know if that really helped, but it made me feel better. The pyramid was now in the center of the screen. Yep, I was going to hit it dead on.

"You have to time this right, scout," Ambassador Plant said.

"He will," GiS, Princess Amana and Kymm all said.

The image of the pyramid shifted in the screen. I tilted the stick a bit to right. The image centered again.

UHF-1 one appeared on the main screen. "Interesting, humans. You have made this quite enjoyable to our viewers."

A few regular TVTrons rolled up to UHF-1. "Sir, we calculate the humans have a 70 percent chance of destroying us."

UHF-1 just smiled. "Ah, the things we do for our viewers."

I made one slight adjustment on the control stick. The pyramid was now dead in my sites.

"Now! Warp!" I shouted.

The small window on the screen was lit up by a fiery explosion. We could only see it for a tic, though, as the image on the main screen inverted. We had escaped into negative space. I exhaled slowly. Our ship rocked up and down. Okay, maybe I exhaled a bit too soon.

"I've never felt hyperspace this bumpy," one of the politicians said.

"We pulled a bit of the explosion's aftershock into hyperspace with us," SC said.

The ship continued to rock and shake.

"I didn't think that was possible," Chriz said.

"Apparently it is," SC said. "Not to worry though. I compute the ship will hold together. Not only that, but we will outrun the shock wave in, three, two, one... Now."

The shaking stopped.

"See," SC said. "I learned the countdown thing from you humans. We are in the clear now."

A cheer erupted. Human and Aquarians started hugging each other. The princess ran up to me and hugged me. "I knew you could do it, Baxter!" she said. Not sure what felt better — being safe, or the hug.

Chapter 22

THE NEXT DAY OR SO PROVED very interesting. On the trip back to Earth, the humans and Aquarians actually got to talk. They made more progress on that one-day trip than they had in weeks of negotiating.

When we got back the station, I was greeted as a hero. Though most of the general population was left in the dark (they didn't want to scare them), word still managed to leak out. At least among the scouts, the troops and the politicians. There were a few politicians who thought that even though I did stop a war from happening, I did it at the cost of a multi-billion dollar Earth ship. Therefore they tried to pass a motion that my pay be docked for well, forever. Luckily the motion was shot down 280 to 20.

The princess had decided to stay on Earth and act as a goodwill ambassador. I was happy about that as she said she would make frequent trips to our base to make sure it was in working order. And well, for other things.

I had learned a lot about myself. I may not have been geneti-cally engineered to be perfect but I still had my own gifts. In fact we all did. I had also learned a lot about my crew and my scout-mates. We were all different. We all had our strengths. We all had a weakness or two. That's why we needed to work together to make each other a little better. Our whole was greater than the sum of our parts. By helping each other we helped the world. By helping the world we helped make the universe better. Isn't that the point of our existence?

"You look tired, Scout," GiS said, as he saw me sitting alone in the mess hall.

"It's been a long last couple of days," I told him as I took a sip of tea.

He looked at his wrist communicator then he looked at me. "It's 23:49, you should be in bed."

I smiled.

"Same old GiS, I see."

GiS actually returned my smile. "Why shouldn't I be? I like me the way I am. I also like the results I get from training you the way I do."

I guess I couldn't argue with that logic. Maybe I could, but it wouldn't do me any good. It was late. I needed to hit the sack. Sure I had been a part of something good, something special. I wasn't the same as I was before the mission, that was true. Heck, it looked like I had a girlfriend, who was a princess from another planet. So things had changed. But I was still me, Baxter Moon, Galactic Scout. GiS was still my superior. I still needed sleep.

I stood up. "You're right, Commander. I'll see you in the morning."

"Yes, bright and early at 0600 hours."

I gave him a polite salute. Which he returned.

I started toward the door.

"Scout Moon," GiS called to me.

I stopped and turned to him. "Yes?"

GiS gave me a nod. "You did good, my boy. You did good. I'm proud of you."

I gave him another salute. "I couldn't have done it without you, my team and a lot of other people."

"Yes, I know, but the important thing is you know that too." He gave me a salute. "Sleep well, Scout. That's an order."

I turned and headed for my room. I felt good, better about myself than I had in a long, long time. I finally knew that this was where I belonged. Better yet, I knew that this was only the start. Things were sure to get even more interesting from here on.

The End

About the author

John Zakour is a humor/sci-fi/fantasy writer with a Master's degree in Human Behavior. He has written zillions (well, thousands) of gags for syndicated comics and comedians (including: *Rugrats, Grimmy, Marmaduke, Bound and Gagged, Dennis the Menace, The Tonight Show* and Joan River's old TV show.) John also writes his own syndicated comic, *Working Daze* for United Media. *Working Daze* appears in papers all over the world (well the US, Scotland, Canada and Taiwan) and has a regular web following with over 50,000 readers. John has been the weekly cartoonist for Geek.com and has sold cartoons or gags to hundreds of journals, magazines and web sites. John also has been a regular contributor to *Nickelodeon* magazine, and to *Fairly Odd Parents, Rugrats* and *Jimmy Neutron* comic books. Starting in 2008, John will be the regular Sunday writer of the *Marmaduke* comic, featured in over 400 papers.

This is his first book for young readers, but his other books include *The Plutonium Blonde, The Doomsday Brunette, The Radioactive Redhead, The Frost Haired Vixen* and *The Blue Haired Bombshell.*

If you'd like to write to him, his email address is *johnzakour@yahoo.com.*